W9-BPN-371

FLOATING

LIKE

THE

DEAD

Floating Like the Dead

YASUKO THANH

Emblem
McClelland & Stewart

Copyright © 2012 by Yasuko Thanh

Emblem is an imprint of McClelland & Stewart Ltd.
Emblem and colophon are registered trademarks of McClelland &
Stewart Ltd.

All rights reserved. The use of any part of this publication reproduced,
transmitted in any form or by any means, electronic, mechanical,
photocopying, recording, or otherwise, or stored in a retrieval system,
without the prior written consent of the publisher – or, in case of
photocopying or other reprographic copying, a licence from the Canadian
Copyright Licensing Agency – is an infringement of the copyright law.

LIBRARY AND ARCHIVES CANADA CATALOGUING IN PUBLICATION
Thanh, Yasuko
Floating like the dead / Yasuko Thanh.

Short stories.
ISBN 978-0-7710-8429-4

I. Title.

PS8639.H375F56 2012   C813.'6   C2011-904270-3

We acknowledge the financial support of the Government of Canada
through the Canada Book Fund and that of the Government of
Ontario through the Ontario Media Development Corporation's
Ontario Book Initiative. We further acknowledge the support of
the Canada Council for the Arts and the Ontario Arts Council
for our publishing program.

The following stories were previously published in a different form:
"Lula May's Love Stories" in *The Fiddlehead*; "Hunting in Spanish"
(as "Leaving Puerto Juarez") in *PRISM international*; and "Floating Like
the Dead" in *Vancouver Review* and *The Journey Prize Stories 21*.

Typeset in Filosofia by M&S, Toronto
Printed and bound in Canada

McClelland & Stewart Ltd.
75 Sherbourne Street
Toronto, Ontario
M5A 2P9
www.mcclelland.com

1 2 3 4 5   16 15 14 13 12

For my parents,
who tell me stories

CONTENTS

Spring-Blade Knife

· 1 ·

Lula May's Love Stories

· 29 ·

Floating Like the Dead

· 48 ·

Hunting in Spanish

· 70 ·

Helen and Frank

· 103 ·

Hustler

· 120 ·

Her Vietnamese Boyfriend

· 149 ·

The Peach Trees of Nhat Tan

· 180 ·

His Lover's Ghost

· 195 ·

Acknowledgements

· 231 ·

SPRING-BLADE KNIFE

I t's a funny thing, to know the exact date of your death. I've
known it for six months, since my sentencing, and hardly
a minute goes by I don't remember it. That was also the day
I was segregated from general population and moved from
South Wing to one of these isolation cells. I was left alone
twenty-three hours a day, but I got two hours outside on
Mondays and Thursdays, in a plotted-off pen, where I could
jog in a circle and breathe air that smelled like apples and
manure from the work yard. They don't put prisoners who've
been sentenced to death back into population; it's bad for
morale, one of the guards told me.

From my cell, all I could hear were the tread of the guards'
boots on the tier, the clink of their keys in the steel doors,
the voices of other inmates whispering or weeping. Then,
two days ago, I got moved to this countdown chamber: six

feet by nine feet, with a mattress and a toilet, where I can only hear the protestors outside. This is where I'll be until tomorrow, June 2, 1948, when I hang.

My name is Mose Donato De Luca and I'm seventeen steps from the gallows. I was named after my grandfather, though The Stranglers called me Doc. My mother calls me Donny. The newspapers have called me a lot of things: a hooligan, a drag-racing punk, and a few other names that aren't worth repeating. But two days ago, Reverend Joseph called me friend as he helped me pack up my things for the move to this last holding cell.

He helped me peel off the walls some sketches I'd made during that time in segregation. I'd drawn the rods outside the Burger Joint: louvered hoods and whacked grilles, headlights streamlined into the fenders, paint and clean sheet metal, all sweetness and light. I'd drawn pictures from my childhood, things I remembered, my old slot cars, our first dog, Crusty. The books that needed to be returned to the prison library, the reverend and I stacked in a corner of the cell. Talking to him eased my mind, like always. The only thing the reverend and I didn't pack was my Bible.

Before Reverend Joseph left, he gave me a medallion, a cross with a circle underneath, and inside the circle were two horizontal lines. I turned the medallion over in my hand and rubbed the bars.

"It means all people are equal," he said, "in God's eyes."

The metal felt cold against my skin. "Equal, huh? Are you sure? I've never seen a millionaire on death row."

But his words got stuck in my head. That night I kept thinking about God's love washing over all men equally.

When I still lived in South Wing, before I was sentenced, I was surrounded by other men awaiting trial. Some of them had only gone to school up to grade three or had stolen their first car at eight or lived on their own since twelve, working the ice rackets or down on the waterfront. I felt guilty around them for having a house and a family. They'd never had a choice and I'd chosen to be a criminal.

I wrote letters for them. They gave me their words for their mothers, or kids, or girlfriends. I read to those who couldn't read and just needed to hear a story, any story, about a blonde, a hot rod, a getaway with a robber to cheer for. I even read some of them scripture, and often enough they started calling me Mr. Bible when they saw me coming down the tier.

The only thing that maybe makes men equal in prison is the limbo we're all in, all of us waiting. It makes me think that maybe hell isn't always a place. Maybe it's a way of feeling right here on earth.

My family wasn't rich, but we were a family like any other. My parents had come from Italy in the late 1920s, right before I was born, and like most immigrants our house wasn't a mansion by any stretch of the imagination. We had oil-cloth floors and floral wallpaper. Before the house on King Edward, we lived on Union Street in Strathcona, not far from Commercial Drive.

No rich people ever lived in Strathcona. None of its people ever made it into the papers for anything good. We lived near the Bancos, the Brunos, the Maltempis. It was as if everyone wanted to find a new life on our east-end Vancouver street. My father worked at a restaurant sixty hours a week, saved his money, and tried to teach us what it meant to work hard for something. But every night he'd come home dead tired and fall into his ratty arm chair. Mom would wait up for him, keeping his dinner plate warm, though sometimes he didn't eat dinner at all because he'd already be asleep with his shoes still on in front of the radio. I'd watch her turning the tuning knob with sadness in her eyes, heaviness in her shuffle as she moved across the room to light a lamp.

I ignored what my dad tried to teach me and instead taught myself how to slip a lock jimmy in between the rubber of a window and a car door, pry the ring off an ignition housing, and cross two terminals to crank an engine. Sometimes a man would hire me to steal a car for twenty-five dollars a pop or sometimes I stole for myself – radio antennas, hubcaps, tires – and sold the parts to dealers and junkies. I didn't steal for the money alone, but for the feel of speed, racing down the road at night, weightless and free. When I smelled the burning rubber, saw the smoke in the rear view, gone was the weight of a life that would steamroll me to a stop. The load flew off me and away during an eighty-mile-an-hour roll.

When I got caught with that first stolen car, my case worker tried to scare me. She said that I was a communist, that Senator Tom Reid thought I was a communist, and that I was going to get two years for hanging out with a gang that had been seen at Party recruitment drives.

"What?" I said. "Call me a dunce. I might not know much about politics, but listen: no Strangler was ever a pinko."

When she didn't shame me straight, the Youth Guidance Division threatened me with twenty months in the Boys' Industrial School. That didn't change my mind about stealing cars either. What nobody understood was that back then I would have done any length of time in prison for my gang. That was years ago, now.

When Culos, Morton, and I hung out, we weren't political. We'd drink espresso shots in Cafe Pingado or go to Ten Pin Alley to bowl or shoot pool at Rocco's. When we were bored, we made gas-pipe blackjacks or wooden clubs or chain knuckle dusters. I'd sit around in a rented room for hours just throwing a spring-blade knife against a wall.

"I got so good I could pin a poker chip at fifteen paces," I told Reverend Joseph, not bragging, but just to show him how I junked my time.

My gang, the Main Street Stranglers, hung around Little Italy on Commercial Drive. We weren't as big a gang as the Capones, our allies, who could fill the entire Burger Joint, but we had a reputation for being tough and I was one of the meanest fighters. "No one gets hurt," was my motto. I was ready to bleed for any Strangler in trouble and every Strangler knew it. But I was crazy enough to fart on demand and had a girlfriend who left me for it, too. Hell, I'd go into a department store and walk out wearing a lampshade on my head if it would give everybody a kick.

On weekends, five or six of us might pile into Culos's hopped-up '32, the one we made from stolen parts hammered together in the hangar on Hastings Street. Maybe three or four other Strangler cars would join us. We'd drive around the community centre looking for our buddies, the Vic Gang, whose territory staked around Victoria Drive, or we'd cruise Broadway looking for our enemies, the Alma Dukes, to wise off, or rumble, or challenge to a drag race.

That night the setting sun shone in the windshield and I tilted my face toward it, to get the last of the heat. Culos was driving, with Morton and Little Nicky in the back.

"We should get some girls," Little Nicky said. He was the youngest of us all, turning fourteen that night, and ready for some fun.

"You know what to do with them?" Morton asked.

"Don't tease the kid," I said.

"More'n you," Little Nicky replied.

"Yeah?" Morton said. "What do you do with them?"

"Look at those eyes," Culos said. "He's a pretty boy. The girls think he's cherry. They know what to do with him."

Saturday night, The Burger Joint would be hopping with girls from the high school who liked leather jackets, and with boys who pretended, a toothpick in their mouth, their eyes half-closed. Not everyone was in a gang, but everyone came knowing something could happen. The electricity in the air tanked you high, like we were tanked full.

Culos had filched some loganberry wine from his parents. We felt good. We felt so good, Morton lit a joint and passed it to me. I took a sharp drag and held the smoke in my lungs.

I turned the radio on and leaned back. Culos stretched one arm over his head and said, "So. Blond or brunette?"

When Morton and Culos talked, their voices sounded like they were coming through a tunnel. It was so funny I laughed. Then I coughed. My eyes watered. Morton said you've got to cough to get off. I passed the joint to Little Nicky, still coughing. Little Nicky passed it to Morton. Morton passed it back to me.

That night the Alma Dukes were there, too, the boys parked on the street and peacocking in front of their rods. Culos, Morton, and I strolled passed them in white buckskin shoes we'd bought on Granville Street in a store where all the hep-cats spent their money. For weeks, we'd been admiring those shoes in the window. "Aren't those zoomy," we'd say when we walked past. We liked to look good, all three of us – I had on an oversized fedora with a wide pinstriped brim and my long, white fingertip jacket – and I guess I was strutting when we passed those Alma Dukes.

Culos slicked back the sides of his greased hair with a comb that he kept in his back pocket. He looked good and I wanted to look good too and I thought after we'd had some fun I'd go down to Modernize, the Chinese tailor shop, maybe even put down a deposit on a new pair of strides.

"Boys. Hey, boys," an Alma Duke with one green eye and one brown one said. He looked down at our shoes. "A little bit jazzy, don't you think?"

"Jazzy? No, I don't think so," I said. I turned to Culos. "Do you? Think they're too jazzy?"

Culos said, "What did he say? Did he just say something to us?"

"I said, did you boys just walk through some flour?"

"Nope, he didn't say nothing," I said and kept walking toward the door.

"If you don't speak up," Culos said, "I'm going to whomp you."

"I repeat," he said, "did you boys just walk through some flour?"

Culos grabbed him. He held onto his jacket and shook him up and down like a sack of potatoes a few times. Then he threw him to the ground and kicked him before he had a chance to get up. Girls came running out to watch. Other boys jumped in.

Fighting made me feel the same way driving fast did – free. I know the others felt it, too, the ones that watched and imagined themselves throwing punches, maybe hitting someone right between the eyes or on that button in the chin with an energetic clip. You could tell they wanted that kind of clean satisfaction, their eyes fairly shone like jewels with the hope and desire of it.

When I glanced up, Culos, sitting on the ground against the curb, catching his breath, winked at me.

Morton was standing in the centre of the tornado and looking around, like he was deciding who to punch next.

Then suddenly I went down and someone in an Alma Duke's jacket was standing over me saying, "You ready for more?"

I tried to stand up but fell down, dizzy. The other guy watched me try to regain my footing. "Come on, buddy. You want?"

"Bastard," I said.

Somehow I got up and we stumbled and kept fighting, along with the rest of the kids who were spilling out the doors. Before it was over, there were more than thirty of us in front of the Burger Joint, everyone punching and biting and spitting, even the girls. Some houses faced the street and an old guy had come out of one of the doorways. He reminded me of my dad and I still get a chill remembering how he looked as he walked around in his pyjamas, the twinge in his voice as he asked us if we'd seen his son. He just kept saying, "I'm looking for my son," over and over, walking around between the fighters, looking lost. I wonder to this day if he ever found him.

Little Nicky had just joined the Stranglers and we wanted to show him a good time. It didn't go that way. Someone pulled a knife.

I saw some kids run to the circle of alder trees next to the parking lot. They waited, watching from there.

Then I heard a kind of wavy "Oooooh" go up from the crowd, kind of rise up from the tops of their heads and then go back down again to the pavement.

Culos and Morton were crouched down beside Little Nicky. "This is no good, Doc, this is no good," Morton said. "It was one of the Alma Dukes."

Culos had his hand over the hole in Little Nicky's chest, but was having a hard time stopping the blood because Nicky was thrashing around so much. I looked down at Little Nicky lying on the pavement in a pool of blood that was growing beneath his body. A girl put her hand over her mouth and threw up between her fingers. The blood pool quickly spread and suddenly we were standing in it, red staining our white shoes.

Red bubbles were coming from Nicky's lips. The sound of the bubbles was strange, especially mixed in with his moaning.

"Little Nicky," I said, bending down. "Who did this? Who pulled a goddamn knife?"

His thrashing became shaking and then the shaking stopped.

We heard the sirens. They couldn't be very far away, and grew louder by the second, piercing the sound of the crowd that had gathered around Little Nicky, encircling him. The yelling, crying, and shouting stopped as everyone looked at each other, deciding what to do. I knew what they were thinking because I thought it, too. Surely an ambulance was among those sirens. We took one last look at Nicky and ran. We ran when we heard the police sirens, but I couldn't get Little Nicky out of my mind, lying in the parking lot.

He spent two weeks in St. Paul's intensive care before going home in ventilator, with a crackle in his chest whenever he breathed.

Besides Reverend Joseph, I don't get a lot of visitors. I've thought a lot about it; how Culos and Morton, who I thought were my brothers, couldn't even visit once. So I was excited when I was told that I had a visitor a couple of weeks ago. But it turned out to be a doctor with the Vancouver Eye, Ear, and Throat Hospital. He was wearing a suit, sweat ringing the collar.

"What I do is help people see again," he said.

"Sorry, Doc, but I have twenty-twenty vision."

"No, Donny. That's not what I meant. Have you heard of organ transplant? I help the blind see again through something called cornea transplantation." He said he gave people a chance at what he called visual redemption.

"You can do that?"

"Scientists can even keep a chicken heart in a machine alive and thriving. One day we'll be able to transplant hearts." He paused for a moment. "Now, I'd like you to consider that you could still do some real good in this world. Which is why I'm here. I'd like to get your consent."

"You saying you want my eyes?"

The doctor cleared his throat. "You could leave a legacy. A legacy of sight. If you were to pledge me your eyes, a part of you would continue to live on after you've died. Think about that, Donny."

After the doctor left, I got my name put on the call list the next day so I could talk to my dad about it.

My dad listened patiently before he told me how he felt. He was afraid I wouldn't be allowed into heaven if my body was in pieces.

"Your mother is suffering already," he said. "Why make it worse?"

My mother. Her cheeks like orange peels, rough yet fragrant. Hands at her throat toying with a necklace. My mother with an umbrella, her stockings wet, by the lilac bush in the backyard that time we'd locked ourselves out of the house and had to wait in the rain for my dad to come home.

I haven't seen her since the trial. I know it was hard for her, the courtroom with all the photographers and reporters, people lining up to get seats. Her eyes welled up every time the prosecutor spoke. My mother, who sang songs in Italian about angels.

"But I'm trying to make it better," I told my dad. "For Mom, and everyone. They'll take my eyes and give them to a little boy. I'm going to help someone see."

"She's happy to hear you're praying again," he said. "We're all happy. But desecrating God's temple . . . You know as well as anyone it's forbidden. It's written in the Bible."

My body hadn't felt like a temple in a long time.

I only hoped my eyes wouldn't carry my memories. There are some things a nine-year-old boy just shouldn't see.

Through my cell window, I could hear the shouts of the protestors outside. They started gathering around the Westgate service exit early this morning, and from the way the shouts were getting louder, I could tell the crowd was growing in number as the day wore on. It was hard to make out exactly what they were saying and sometimes I wondered if they all wanted me to hang, or if there were maybe some of them who didn't. After the quiet of the last six months, hearing their constant chanting made my hands jittery. I had to do something to keep them busy, so I asked Constable Willard for some soap.

"You got your whatnot for washing in there already, don't you?"

"And some water. I want to wash my cell."

"What for?" he said, but he brought me soap and a bucket of water, too.

I washed the walls and the floor of my cell until my hands were bleeding and Constable Willard finally told me to stop. We'd talked a couple of times since Monday. He seemed like a decent guy, not like some of the guards I'd seen on South Wing who'd whip a man for the sheer pleasure of the crack of leather in the air.

Now he set up a poker game for us, trying to distract me. "Don't forget, your family's coming soon," he said.

I sat down and we played between the bars, him sitting at

his table outside my cell, me perched at the end of my cot that was nailed to the wall.

Constable Willard looked to be about the same age as my dad and when I asked him how long he'd been working here, he had to think for a moment before he said he'd been at Oakalla for twenty-five years. "I guess you could call me a lifer, too."

"So, you believe . . . in this?"

"I've seen over forty executions," Constable Willard said, "for whatever that's worth, and I remember all of them. I believe in the law."

"Are you a Christian man, Constable Willard?"

"Call me Frank," he said.

The chanting outside was getting louder and I thought I was going to explode. I swear I heard someone say, "Choke the dirt" or "Choke the jerk." I looked away from the window trying to focus my attention away from the chanting and onto the cards in my hand.

"Do you have faith?" I asked him.

"Sure," he answered. I could tell from the puzzled look on his face he didn't know what I was getting at. "You ask funny questions, son."

"How do you know? I mean, how do you know you have faith?"

He started dealing another hand. "Faith . . . is faith. It's not a question of knowing. I don't have to think about it."

On the wall next to my bed, I happened to notice a mark, maybe the beginning of an A, someone's initial. It looked like someone had scratched it into the wall and I wondered who it was.

"Did you play cards with all the men?" I asked Frank.

"Some men would've liked to smash me over the head with this table soon as sit with me at it."

"Well, I wouldn't do that to you," I said. I meant my voice to sound reassuring. It came out sounding pleading, like I was trying to prove something. So I tried again: "You believe me, though, that I wouldn't do that to you."

"I wouldn't be sitting here otherwise."

We played poker until another guard told us my family had arrived. Before we went into the visiting room, Frank told me the rules. "One kiss and one hug at the start of the visit. One kiss and one hug at the end. You can hold hands with your folks so long as you keep your hands where I can see them."

"Even though I'm wearing cuffs? You kidding?"

My father and my little sister Sophia were inside, but not my mother.

My dad got mad about the handcuffs on my wrists. "Why does he got those for? He can't run away."

"Don't do that to him," I said. "He's a good man. He just has his orders."

I tried to lighten the mood by pointing to the name sewn onto my prison jacket, which says Deluca. "They still haven't changed the spelling."

"You think if they're going to kill a man they could at least get his name right," my dad said.

My dad was wearing his hat with the fishing pins. He took it off and wrung it in his hands. My sister Sophia stood looking at her saddle shoes. She'd placed a yellow rose through the buttonhole of her dress.

"Is that from Mom's garden?" I asked her.

She nodded. Her eyes were bloated from crying.

"Where's Mom?"

Sophia looked away.

Dad put his hand on top of mine. He swallowed, holding himself in. It broke my heart to think of my mother curled into her slippery turquoise robe, unable to get out of bed because of the grief I've caused her.

My dad said, "How are you holding up?"

"Holding," I said.

I know this waiting can be a strain for some prisoners. We sat down and I told him it just about drove one guy so crazy he tried to kill himself before the guards came to take him to the gallows. And another inmate, a man who's been in here for thirty years, can't even walk to the showers by himself. He's too old and frail to comb his own hair.

"I don't want to die like that, wanting to slit my neck, or so old that I want to trade this concrete coffin for a real one."

Sophia sat down and covered her eyes with her hands. "There's got to be something," she said desperately. "Another appeal. There's got to be someone who can help."

"There's nothing," my dad said in a quiet voice.

"It's not fair," Sophia said. "Justice is a joke." She shook her head. "I don't understand. How did any of this happen?"

I shook my head. "I killed a man," I said, not looking up.

"So killing you makes it right?"

"Sophia," my dad said. "Let's talk about something else."

My dad wiped his nose with his sleeve and from his wallet he pulled out a picture of me in the airplane ride at the Happyland midway. I must have been about ten. There was a chain-swing ride behind me. In the background I can see the top of a circus tent.

Until I was twelve, we'd go to Happyland once a year and I was keen to stroll through the park, eating corn dogs and winning at the midway games. Happyland closed with the war in 1941. When it reopened five years later, nothing was the same: I was living in flop rooms, jacking cars, hoboing around with the gang, and visiting my folks maybe only once every couple of months.

One of my fondest memories of Happyland is watching a military parade from my father's shoulders. I would have been about ten at the time, but I was heavy and big for my age. Still, he lifted me as high as his shoulders could take me. I felt like a pilot; I felt like the earth and the sky and everything in between belonged to me

"You cried when you saw the Alligator-skinned man," I said to Sophia.

Sophia went, "Haaa," a gentle exhalation, not a laugh or a cry, maybe something in between.

I leaned forward and touched her arm. "You okay?" I said.

"How can they do this to you — kill the part of you that has those memories?" The word *memories* seemed to spurt up from somewhere deep inside her and I could tell from the way she was trembling that she was trying to stop the flow of anguish.

"I'm sorry," she said, "for crying. I want to be strong."

"Don't be sorry."

"I am sorry. I am. Because . . . there's no death in God, only salvation."

"Sophia."

"I'm sorry." She patted my hand. "I'm sorry." Then she looked me deep in the eyes and her *I'm sorry*'s became *sorry*'s not just for herself but for me and all of humanity, the whole sorry lot of us.

Frank took her out of the visiting room, leading her by the hand.

I felt as helpless as the time she fell while I was teaching her how to ride her first bike. Her tooth had gone through her upper lip, but before the blood appeared, there was this moment when her tooth was just a tooth in a bed of red lip, and I felt like I could still save her from the pain. Of course, nothing I could do would stop the blood from spilling. Nothing I said could take away her anguish.

When she left the room, my dad asked me, "Have you prayed? I mean really?"

"Sometimes there's no words," I said. "Just emptiness inside."

We bowed our heads and prayed. "Jesus have mercy on us, God have mercy on us, Christ have mercy on us, *abbi misericordia di me peccatore.*"

I don't know how much time passed. When I looked up, my sister had returned.

"God's will is the important thing," I said. "What I want doesn't matter. God is going to make sure something good comes of my death." It was hard not to choke on the words, I so wanted to believe them. But I would hold in my tears — I had already hurt my family too much.

"God loves you," my dad said. "You've got nothing to prove."

"It's not that," I said. Watching him like that, his shoulders hunched, his eyes red-rimmed, his cheeks nicked with little shaving cuts — it made me want to curl up inside.

"I'm so angry right now," Sophia said. "I don't know if it will ever go away."

It hit me, then, truly, what I'd done. I wanted to tell her the last thing I'd be thinking about was how we used to sit on the banks of the Fraser and toss stones at the log booms. Or that time we found two rough-winged swallows just hatched, these little balls of down, in a mud-and-twig nest in the corner of our front porch. I tried to say something, but she was crying again and then I got to thinking that maybe I couldn't tell her without making things worse. What was the point of returning to a place that no longer existed except in your head?

Dad tried to smile. "Is there anything I can do for you?" he asked.

"Stop crying and sit up straight," I said.

"But you're my little boy."

We visited for five hours.

Before they left, feeling my father's body close to mine made me think of the days he worked at the restaurant, how he would come home with the smell of salami on his clothes. I stepped back and held his hands at an arm's length. "Don't watch me hang," I said, surprised by my words.

He let go and I think he was as shocked as me. He had the look of someone with a knife to his throat.

Panicked, I wanted to reach out and put my hand on his shoulder, but in that moment my arms didn't feel like they could change anything. I was made of shadows and smoke.

The deepest injuries are those we inflict on our loved ones.

But he can't watch me die – people get lost in that kind of pain, and I don't know if anyone can ever love you back out of something like that.

Back in my cell, I sat on my bed and didn't move. Frank got out the cards and shuffled the deck around, trying to get me to talk.

I didn't even look at him. If I could just sit still long enough, maybe I could hold the memory of my family's visit inside, the way a car left out all day in the sun holds the heat and won't let go, keeping the warmth inside long after night has fallen.

It's custom to give a man a shot or two of brandy in the hours leading up to his execution, if there happens to be a bottle. It's called the therapeutic dosage and Frank told me that once he ran all the way home because there was no brandy in the jail. I haven't asked for any.

I won't ask. I want to stay in charge of my mind.

I want to keep my memories, even the ones I'd rather not remember. Maybe especially what I don't want to remember. I don't deserve to forget.

It was the Thanksgiving Day long weekend. Inside the Happyland dancehall, I was hugging up on that girl with the Rita Hayworth hair and the yellow dress that rustled. For the second time that night the band played "Smoke! Smoke! Smoke! That Cigarette."

Then Morton ran inside and yelled from the door to *Come on, come on,* the Alma Dukes had got Culos.

In the end, I kicked a guy in the parking lot and he went down. I kicked him again. I thought I was being a hero, but he wasn't even an Alma Duke. I just saw the image of Little

Nicky lying on the pavement and I lost myself. The adrenalin was steel in my veins. I kicked a man to death.

I heard the bones on the side of his head crack in. The sound was loud, louder than you'd think. I must have been using his head like a soccer ball pretty good because later my foot hurt. In my head I kept saying, "This one's for Little Nicky," but maybe I yelled it a couple times too. Some of his hair was stuck to my boot. The blood still felt warm when I brushed the hair off later. It wasn't me at all.

His name was Freddy St. Laurent and I found out at the trial he was a boxer. Nothing I say or do can ever stop my mind from imagining his fear, or what he felt as I kicked him, knowing I wasn't going to stop. I can still see him lying there, looking up at me, and what he saw was worse than a blur of boot covered with his own blood, worse than the exploding fireworks that came with the sickening smack when that boot hit his temple. What he saw was something already dead, the nothingness in my eyes as cold and deep as outer space.

Yesterday the hangman came to measure me.

"For a hanging to work right," he said, "the rope has to be stretched for two years to take out its spring."

He weighed me carefully so he could select the proper length.

Constable LaShelle took his hands out of his pockets and flipped his chin. "You practise with potato sacks first?" His eyes were gleaming with the hard shine of blue marbles.

The hangman glanced up from the scale. His face was sharp, as if he didn't like having to explain himself. "Flour," he said, and looked down again. "I use flour sacks for practice."

"I heard about this mistake," LaShelle said. "This huge guy, this prisoner, must've been 250 if he was a pound. When the rope went taut, his head popped off."

The hangman gave the constable a look, a wave of something like pity sweeping over his face. It reminded me of how you might look at a dog run over by a car, with a mixture of sympathy and disgust.

I didn't sleep much last night.

Before my father and sister left, they gave me another picture. It was of the family standing in front of the new house on King Edward just a few months before I got arrested. I had come home for Easter, my first visit since Christmas. Thinking back on it now, it was the last time we were all together, before the trial.

My sister is holding the box of chocolates I brought her. I'd looked at all the boxes in the drugstore down the street, trying to find the cheapest one — I only bought one box, thinking my mother and sister could share. They'd kissed me on both of my cheeks when I gave it to them. I hated myself, thinking of it.

In my hand, I'm holding my childhood Bible, the white one I'd gotten for memorizing the twenty-third Psalm and reciting it in front of my Sunday-school class.

I remember underlining lots of verses in red pencil when I was still in elementary school. "Blessed are they that mourn: for they shall be comforted."

I have a real Bible now. I've held this Bible, trying to remember the way I'd felt reading my white Bible as a kid, trying to get back to that place, that feeling of certainty, as solid and unwavering as an iron bridge.

But I can't. One minute Freddy St. Laurent was still alive and the next he lay curled on the pavement, one eye wide open, staring at me into forever. That split second turned me into who I'll be the rest of my life; who my parents will remember for the rest of theirs; who the news clippings put down forever in black and white. When I think about that moment, something overwhelms me and I have to go inside myself. I've sat in my cell for days, not saying anything to anyone, waiting for all the shame to pass through me.

But I can't get rid of the feeling that the moment before still exists somewhere. That, if I could only get back to that moment, that split second of possibility, before everything went wrong, then maybe a part of me might be worth saving. The part of me that looked at the just-hatched swallows in a twig nest on our family's porch or watched my parents, tall beside me, singing hymns on Sunday. I was a part of something good and pure back then. Maybe, if I could just get back there, that kernel of me might be worth saving. Might even be worth giving to someone else.

After my family left, I ate my last meal. It was my favourite meal: a fried garlic and potato omelette with sliced tomatoes. For dessert, I wanted a piece of cheesecake. The dinner wasn't like how my mom would have made it because the kitchen had run out of garlic, so it was just potato in the omelette. And the cheesecake was the frozen kind, but it was still good.

Reverend Joseph sat beside me the entire time and patted my arm, assuring me he wasn't going anywhere. He is a small man, skinny, with the kind of sucked-in cheeks that give the impression he's taking a drag on a cigarette. He's got thin hair and thin shoulders. I have a hard time imagining him doing stuff like buying groceries, driving a car, or cleaning his toilet. The job must take it out of him, I thought, because he looks like he has one foot in the grave himself.

It was tricky to balance my plate on my lap while I ate because the holding cell doesn't have a table. I didn't know where to put down my knife except on the cot. Thinking I was getting close to my last bite made it even harder to eat. That's when I looked down at my meal and made a guess at how many bites I had left. I doubled the number, taking smaller bites, so I could make what was left of my time last as long as possible.

Suddenly, I realized I'd finished half my meal. I'd eaten half my meal and not even tasted it. I put the food down next to me on the bed and cried.

Reverend Joseph put his hand on my shoulder. He just let me cry.

"Can I ask you something straight?" I said.

"Of course, Donny. Anything."

"Do you know where my body is going?"

"I know you've asked for your eyes to be donated. I know about the little boy."

"That's not what I mean. I mean do you know, am I going to heaven, if I've found God? Do you have proof of it?"

"It's written in the Bible that 'whosoever believeth in Me shall not perish, but have everlasting life.'"

I started laughing so hard I almost threw up. It reminded me of being tickled, that kind of uncontrollable laughter. I don't know where it came from. And then it was gone.

A feeling came over me that I needed to see my mom more than anything. "Get my mom on the phone. Rev, call her."

"I'll see what I can do."

"Get my mom. I can't go without seeing my mom."

Frank stuck his head in. "Everything okay?"

"We're okay," Reverend Joseph said, "aren't we, Donny?" He rubbed my back. He nodded at Frank. "We're okay. We'll get your mom."

"My mom, my mom." I rocked back and forth, the feeling I needed her like a live wire inside me, burning me from my heart to my fingertips, thrashing me whole.

"Don't worry," the reverend said.

Frank let him out and he left and I settled back down on the bed.

I felt better knowing he was taking care of it, that she would come. If I could just see her again she'd make everything okay. If she would just put her arm around my shoulder, I knew I could do it: I could walk those seventeen steps without fainting. I knew if she whispered "Everything is going to be okay" into my ear, it would be.

Reverend Joseph came back. His face looked mixed-up, like he didn't know what to tell me. I guess he decided on the truth because finally he said, "I've got some bad news, Donny. Your mom's not coming."

I thought I'd heard wrong. "What do you mean she's not coming?"

He sat down beside me and put his hand on my back.

"What do you mean?" I kept saying.

I felt everything rush out of me like air from a balloon. Two hours left and now there was nothing but the waiting; I'd rather be dead if this is how I was going to feel.

"I wish I could have one more piece of cheesecake,"

I said. "One more piece of cheesecake. One more of anything. You think they'll give it to me?"

Waves of sadness then numbness ran through my body,
one after the other. Maybe these waves would wash me
clean. Maybe they'd pulverise me, grind me down to the size
of a stone, then a pebble, not stopping till I was as invisible
as a grain of sand.

"I wish we could just get it over with," I said quietly.

"Soon," Reverend Joseph said. "It'll all be over soon."

The walls were closing in, and the bed, an open jaw, was
waiting to snap. Even the blankets wanted to strangle me. I
grabbed one in both hands and pulled against the weave of
the fabric as hard as I could, trying to rip it, kill it first. It
stretched, but didn't give. I tried again and again. Exhausted,
I crumpled back down onto the bed, my body shaking.
Reverend Joseph put the blankets around my shoulders.

"What exactly does, 'It'll be over soon' mean?" I said.
"Over for who? And what? What'll be over? The pain, the
sadness that people can do this to each other, this feeling
like an ice pick in my stomach? Can somebody explain it to
me? What about you, Reverend? Can you explain it to me?
Can you? Come on, I want you try."

He let me carry on, and then when I was quiet again, he said,
"Would you like me to read you something from the Bible?"

"No. Tell me a story."

"Let's see. When I was a young man with the seminary,
I got fed up with the system and decided I wanted to go to
Brooklyn to minister in the streets, to people who really
needed it. I was tired of writing term papers on subjects that
seemed so far away from the actual practice of ministering.

I worked with a youth group and took kids camping. I worked in a kitchen and made terrible soup."

"Tell me *something*. Give me something to focus on, now."

"I'm not sure I know what you mean."

"Anything. What you ate or drank. What did you see? Did you see a sunset?" I kept going. "Or train tracks. I like train tracks. I never been on a train before. Um, teeter totters, my sister and me. Popsicles. Birds, the little ones. Flies in the summer. They stick to the window and their wings glint in the sun."

"Balloons."

"Corn dogs."

"The world can be beautiful, can't it?" he said.

I nodded. Then he read to me from Paul's words in Romans, "'For I am certain of this: neither death nor life, no angel, no prince, nothing that exists, nothing still to come, not any power or height or depth, nor any created thing, can ever come between us and the love of God.'"

"Life in Jesus Christ," he said. "Life everlasting."

"Well, I think that some people can live more than one life."

"You mean reincarnation?" he said. "It's not what the church believes."

"No. I think some people can live more than one life. Some people can live many lives in just one existence."

He helped me pin the two photographs of Happyland onto my chest over my front pocket, where I'd put the medallion he'd given me. Then he listened as I talked about my family. I told him about how before we had a car, my father rode a bicycle and my mother used to sit on the rat-trap. Whenever we rode to the Little League diamond on Turner Street, across from the raceway, I felt nothing but embarrassed that a friend from school would see me, sitting there on the bicycle, wedged between the two of them, that close to my mom and dad.

Around the same time, I used to wear a yellow jacket. I don't know why but one day I wanted an Indian head on the back. Mom bought some fabric, cut out the shape of a head, and stayed up all night sewing it on so I could wear it to school the next day.

I told him about how walking home from school, I would collect dead bees from the gutter. I thought their bodies looked like jewels. I carried them home, cupping them in my hand so their wings wouldn't be damaged, and put them in a jar. I loved to open the jar and breathe in the scent of their bodies, which even in death smelled like honey.

"Donny."

"Yes."

"It's time."

I nodded. We stood up and I grabbed both of the reverend's hands, hard. "Okay."

"Okay," he whispered.

"Okay," but I couldn't let go.

We stood like that until Frank said something about procedures and how the reverend needed to get into the viewing box.

"I'll see you soon," the reverend said again.

And then he was gone. Soon, the hangman will come. He and Constable Willard will escort me from my cell to the execution chamber where reporters, witnesses, and Reverend Joseph will be waiting. Will my father be there? I hope so, now. If I see him in the window, I'll give him the thumbs up to show him I can do this. I'll try to wink – it's all I've got left. I can give him this memory, of me trying to be a good sport, even though I had nothing left to lose.

Prison guards will stand along the hallway marking my seventeen steps. Someone, maybe Frank, will have thrown roses or yellow irises on the floor. The hangman told me a guard had once done this for a man who was a gardener and now the other guards kept the tradition going for certain inmates, because they liked the ritual of it.

Will I be able to walk or will they have to get the gurney? Will I know that I'm falling when the trap door swings open? Will it hurt to die?

I begin to panic, then, and so I try to remember my mother's face. Not the way I saw it last in court, when the prosecutor was speaking, and she looked older and more scared than I had ever seen her look before, but her face the way it used to look, when she was standing at the stove, an apron tied around her waist, stirring the hot chocolate she made me every day after school.

When Reverend Joseph mentioned the blind boy, I thought about my eyes.

I'm happy the boy is nine. He'll see things I could never even imagine. And he'll see light for the first time. Sunshine when it sparkles on the ocean, a pretty girl's dress when she's waiting for you to dance. I hope. And I hope that maybe God will let me see the light too, when it's time to let the breath go.

LULA MAY'S LOVE STORIES

—◦◦◦◦—

R ound and round Clovis spun the steering wheel, every time framing new hills in the windshield, creating a whole new sky – he could do that, easy as a twist. Lula May held her stare on the yucca flowers blooming pink along the highway toward the Brownsville border crossing, growing the same way they did in Hatch. It made her feel better knowing that even here, so close to Mexico, there was something of home; even here it was possible to find something she loved, if only the small yucca blossoms belonging to nobody but the hills.

"Try to love small, Lula May," her mother had warned her. "If you love small, you can keep it safe inside you like a secret. Love too big and it can get away from you."

Clovis was laughing the way he was liable to at nothing in particular. The Valium he'd foolishly bought on a street corner in San Antonio on their way to the border was hidden in the glove box.

It was all happening too fast and Clovis was driving her away in his pickup truck like he used to on Sundays, except now she could imagine his I-can-take-you-anywhere hands being just as likely to hold a .38 to someone's head as to lay a white cloth over a dead bird, something she had once seen him do. That was the Clovis she loved. She tried hard to remember loving him, the way she had yesterday. But now when she looked at him, all she could see was the milky spittle gathered in the corners of his mouth, and his stubble so rough and mean-looking.

No, it wasn't just that he looked mean now. Her second thoughts had started before, with Miss Sugar, the town florist. On regular days, Lula May had seen her standing in front of her shop on Merchant Street, smoking and flicking her ashes into a little artichoke-shaped ceramic planter. Lula May blamed Miss Sugar for being the one Clovis picked — because she was so pretty, because her cherry-patterned dress billowed red. What a fool thing Clovis had done, taking her for a hostage.

Clovis and Lula May would be in Panama by now if Miss Sugar hadn't started all the trouble. Instead, sheer cliffs the colour of a dusty brown dog loomed in the pocked windshield, and along the road grew mesquite trees where black vultures clumped together above the leaves of desert holly pointed brazenly as hands at the sun and the open sky.

No, even that wasn't true. Miss Sugar didn't start *all* the trouble. To get to where the trouble really began Lula May needed to go back as far as her parents' farm, and even to Hatch itself, where, until the robbery, she had lived with her parents and her six brothers and sisters. Along the fractured roads, farmhouses were strung like broken teeth and separated by spines of rusty wire fence, white Dutch clover blooming along dry river beds. The clover had once been sown as forage for cattle and still thrived in the vacant lots and railroad rights-of-way near Elkins Road. Elkins Road, which paused briefly at her family's farmhouse before rambling on, finally plunging into red earth and a rearing, infinite sky. In Hatch, the sky was so open that people planted stands of trees around their houses just to protect themselves from the blue.

At dusk, the air cooled, the glaring pebbles faded into softness, the heat of the day forgotten. But evening's softness brought with it another kind of forgetfulness, which drifted through the catclaw, whitebrush, and guajillo, and was as lethal and impossible to notice as a poisonous gas. The sky would continue to grow a deeper blue, the house sinking into the dusk. And the coolness would make her pause, and it would make her want to sit on the tire swing that hung from the Chinese tallow tree and stare at the swelling sky of stars. She could feel a pull as if from the land itself — roots binding her limbs, tendrils looping through her fingers; a life that, if she sat there long enough, would pick her clean, her bones left to bleach in the unforgiving sun.

She was sick of the backbreaking, sweaty work of tending beehives and the companion struggle to keep the bees healthy. She was sick of counting screened bottom boards and hive boxes and sending the queens in separate packages to Chicago or Navasota, because until the bees got used to a new queen, they would be as likely to kill her as to protect her. Last week she'd been stung again and had to use a knife blade to remove the barb from the back of her hand. She'd dulled the pain with ice, but it made her think of Clovis Peach as her ticket out of this infernal existence.

Clovis Peach had the power to open something inside her that had been waiting like a seedpod for the trigger of the first drops of rain. He was a twenty-first-century pioneer, a miner working in the foothills of Buckeye Mountain not far from her pop's farm, forging new ground. He had the kind of pure unbidden smile that made women and men smile back with genuine happiness. Val the cashier did, as did Lula May, the day she met Clovis at the Trading Post two months ago when she was skipping school. She had noticed his hard-working hands buying bacon and soap – hands she imagined fixing things, uncovering gold, and building a home where nothing had stood before.

"I'm going to be rich," he'd told her. "And you will have luxury. Stick with me, Princess." He winked. "Just watch what happens."

From the first time she met him she just knew they'd love each other forever. Clovis Peach made her a woman.

He was the wisest person she had ever known: "If you're not in control of what's around you, you're as good as a hunk of wood in the river, letting the current butt you around." Then he'd pick his teeth with a bowie knife, pull out a piece of food with his fingers. "Sometimes a person feels like a wild animal that's been caged for a long time. They go crazy in there, in their cage, pacing back and forth all day, doing figure eights. And what's more, if they're ever let out, they don't run, they just keep pacing, as if the cage was still there. That's never going to happen to you or me, Lula May." At the end of the day she'd happily listen to him talk and talk into the night.

Most evenings, she'd boil the water she carried in soda bottles to Clovis's shack from Superstition River, make coffee, and cook eggs and hash browns for him because that's all the food he ever had, breakfast fixings. Clovis had no electricity or running water. The abandoned two-room pine shack he'd moved into was cozy, even with gaps between the slats and hillocky wood knots on the wall inside. Some of the knots jutted out and were sturdy enough to hang things on: a ten-pound bag of brown potatoes, a coil of nylon rope. He had a single bed made of sweetgum. Soot spilled up the walls above the candles on his nightstand. When the rains came, ceiling drips that sounded musical filled the rusty coffee tins – *ker-plink* – on the hard-packed dirt floor.

In the beginning she hiked to Clovis's shack at least once and sometimes twice a day. Like buried treasure, she used to think, the way his shack hid itself in the rambling hills. Hiking out on the trail from town to see him, she hugged the dry stone walls of the old, pioneer mule tracks lined with sagebrush. Sometimes she daydreamed about getting lost and never being able to find her way out. It would be so easy to confuse this pine for that one or this big rock for any other. What would she do? Would she survive? When she got there, Clovis would be working down the hard stony places, chipping handfuls of the mountain with nothing but faith and a rusty pickaxe. No high-school boy – with their dull homeroom eyes and pimple-faced stares – would ever have done such a thing. Which one of them would have bought mining tools – nearly antique! – from the pawnshop in town with their government welfare cheque and dreamed up the idea of finding gold where none existed. That took guts. To believe you could change things.

But Buckeye Mountain didn't yield its gold, keeping it locked from Clovis. Then, after the accident, he seemed defeated. A candle had tipped over while they slept. He'd tried to extinguish the fire, carrying water from the river in the coffee tins, his fingers blistering from the heat of the flames. But the fire went out when it pleased and paid no attention to Clovis, who, when it was all over, was insulted and hurt.

Instead of soldiering on, he wallowed in the foul-smelling shack, soot on his forehead, the walls still smoking. "What kind of place was this shack if I want to make you my wife? If I had money for real tools – aw, but you already know that."

Lula May set to work making two piles, separating what had been burned from what was still good. Clovis looked more pathetic than he had any right to, and she couldn't decide if she should rub his back or slap him. The fire hadn't killed them, and who was he to sit there moping. Lula May knew they were pioneers in a boundless land of untamed hills and coyotes: "You got to not give up," she said.

She didn't care that her parents had threatened to call the police: her brother Caleb had told her they were getting right fed up with her neglecting the observation hive they were planning to bring to the Pasadena Strawberry Festival, where people would press their faces against the glass walls and peer at all the bees trapped inside. Lula May had already decided she wasn't going to California this year. She was tired of giving out honey samples and answering questions: "Do I have to keep the hive outside or can I keep it in my house?" "If the bees die, do you give refunds?" She had nothing to say to people interested in seeing the world's largest strawberry shortcake, a 1,900-square-foot monstrosity covered with more than a tonne of strawberries and acres of glaze and whipped cream. Let her mother go with one of her other sisters this year. Let her parents threaten to call the police on her if she kept seeing Clovis and cutting school.

"I'm getting rid of the tools," he said. "That's it. It's on to plan B."

She loved him to pieces. To death. Anyone would have. You had no choice when it came to someone like Clovis Peach.

Lula May had been inside shelling peas for her mother when she saw Clovis on their wooden porch. Her mother, who was giving Lula May's youngest sister a bath, was still in earshot, so Lula May snuck out onto the porch and shut the screen door quietly behind her.

"Git, Clovis! My mom's home. And she wasn't kidding when she said she'd call the cops the next time she saw you wolfing around our house."

"Guess you're wondering what I'm doing here," Clovis said, smiling a crazy ear-to-ear grin. A feverish feeling rose in her at the sight of his torn clothes. "Lula May," he whooped, "I robbed the City Trust."

She almost dropped her basket of peas.

"I got a surprise for you, but you got to come quick."

He dragged her by the hand away from home and through alfalfa pastures and flowering brush, in the direction of his shack.

"I thought it would be easier to get back across the river if I had a hostage," Clovis said. "They wouldn't call the cops if I had the girl with me."

But a little voice inside her said, wouldn't it be harder to get across the river with a hostage? Wouldn't the cops be more likely to chase you if you've kidnapped someone? He nearly ripped her elbow out of its socket yanking her down through the hill trails.

"A hostage?" she said.

"Yup. Miss Sugar."

The bank had wide, easy doors laid into a smooth stone front, cool as ice and just as slick, with a handful of low steps leading up to it from the sidewalk. Its friendly scents of writing paper and drugstore perfume were nothing like the wild loamy smell of Clovis's land.

When he reached the top step, Clovis took the gun from his waistband and stepped forward to stake his claim. He pushed through the doors and fired a warning shot into the air.

On his way out of the bank, as an afterthought, he grabbed Miss Sugar around the waist and held her to him, pressing the muzzle of the gun against her ribs. (Lula May could see her creamy hands helplessly gripping the counter, her sloping cow eyes when she realized what was happening. No, no, no, noooooo.) The keys to her flower shop jingled as Clovis spun her out the door as if they were dancing.

On the other side of the river, they hiked through clumps of paloverde, pushing and panting until their teeth ached. Clovis pretending he wasn't lost, putting on invincible airs for Miss Sugar. Finally, they made it to his shack.

"See?" he whooped, pushing the solid sorghum stalks aside. "Told you so," he said. "Right where I said it would be."

Clovis pushed open the door to his shack and, at first, in the dim light, Lula May could not make out the shape of Miss Sugar, lying on her side, gagged and hog-tied on his single bed. There was a cut on her cheek.

When Lula May saw that she was hurt, she fetched some rags, poured the remaining water from the soda bottles into a pot, and set it to boil. Tried to make herself believe this wasn't happening. She carried the steaming pot water over to the table beside the bed, sat down next to Miss Sugar, and placed a dampened cloth against her cut.

"Clovis, you can't do this." Her voice was so low, so foreign, she scared herself.

"What's with you, Lula May? I thought you'd be happy. Now I can buy you all the nice things you ever wanted." He stopped to massage his forehead, as though his plan for the next twenty minutes could be rubbed down from there.

She leaned over the bed where Miss Sugar lay slumped on her side. "Please, don't worry," she whispered into the woman's ear. "Everything's going to be okay."

"Get away from her. Go get the truck."

"What?"

"I ain't saying it twice."

"Where is it?"

"I left it on Taylor Ridge." He narrowed his eyes into slits. "You want the cops to come?"

She thought about it. She hadn't asked him why he'd robbed the City Trust. She didn't want to know if he had done it for her, though of course he had. He loved her.

Lula May felt angry at Miss Sugar without knowing why.

Clovis shoots his gun at the ceiling then makes his way to the teller's window. With the money in hand, he grabs Miss Sugar and pulls her up off the floor, where she had fallen to her knees and thrown her arms over her head at the bang. He is a man sweeping her off her feet, out the door, past the town, into woods of thorny scrub and sagebrush.

When they get to Superstition River, Clovis hand-over-hands his getaway raft, the cord tied tight, to this end a post, to that end a boulder. Miss Sugar just gapes at the river, her pinky-pink lipstick smeared. The water is black. She sits — not fussing, not fighting — on the edge of the raft, her backbone limp with despair.

Sitting on top of her hands.

Wondering how it would feel to jump in.

Miss Sugar feels a chill looking into the blackness. Because water so beautiful, so deep and sweet, made dying seem like a cinch.

"It must've been a cinch," Lula May said, motioning with her chin, "getting her over on the raft like, no trouble."

"You'd think, huh?" Clovis picked at his teeth with his pinkie nail, which was jagged and dirty. "Looking at her, thin and innocent-looking, but, no, she was a handful. More than I bargained for."

Lula May rethought the river, Miss Sugar, too, and made them both rougher.

Clovis tugs Miss Sugar through town, past the weather-beaten buildings, past Ed's Hardware, past Chicken City. He doesn't stop when she trips him up, only yanks her pretty lily-white arm harder over dust whirls and pebbles.

Superstition River is swollen with dead branches and full of sharp-slice rocks, splitting in half anything softer than a stone. Miss Sugar digs her heels into the snakeweed along the river-bank, and even manages to twist away. But he catches her in a split second, as easy as if she were a child. Lula May pictures Clovis fighting the current, his arms heaving them across, his dirty white T-shirt clinging to his muscles. Town buildings fall into shadow behind the reeds.

Miss Sugar: Let me go once we get to the other side.

You won't need me.

Don't kill me.

We could make a deal.

"Okay, I get it. You might not like what you see. But I'm telling you, it's just a little blood."

"Why? Did she fall?"

"Yeah, I guess she fell some."

"Must've been those shoes." Lula May snapped her fingers. "Imagine, those fancy high-heel shoes in the woods."

"Lula May, she put me on the spot. I had to get us across the river, but she wouldn't sit still, wouldn't keep her mouth shut. I couldn't figure her. I never wanted to get violent, never with a woman. I *had* to get us across the river. She *made* me have to settle her down."

She re-imagined Miss Sugar pacing the edges of the raft, cussing and calling Clovis the most stupid bank robber in history, as if eager to get herself pistol-whipped.

With all her might Miss Sugar comes up behind Clovis and pushes him, futilely willing her ninety-eight-pound frame to be enough to launch him overboard. Later, she grabs the gunny sack with the money and threatens to drop it into the deepest part of the Superstition. (Still Miss Sugar doesn't get that Clovis is running the show.) That's when he splits her cheek open with the butt of the .38.

Lula May could have helped her get away. She could have untied the knot, untied the knot, untied the knot. Instead, Lula May got the truck.

∞

Away and away Clovis twisted the steering wheel, each turn taking them closer to the border and farther away from the clearing off the empty stretch of highway where they'd let Miss Sugar go. The sack of stolen money was hidden under the seat, an inch behind the heel of Lula May's boot. The truck roared past cinder-block houses with horse corrals and barns set back from the road and hung with chicken-hawk carcasses. She crossed her fingers: *Someone stop us, please.* The hills came rolling, rolling, rolling out before her eyes and the world seemed unreal – a love story gone wrong with her plopped right in the middle. She squinted at Clovis: banks, hostages, getaways. Never in her craziest imaginings had she ever dreamed of this much trouble.

She played with the door lock, opening and closing it. "So how far south are we going?" she asked.

"I don't know. Costa Rica. Panama. I reckon as far as we can get." He leaned his head toward the open window, blowing out cigarette smoke.

As they neared the Brownsville border crossing, approaching the bridge that joins Texas to Tamaulipas, Clovis said the police would not be expecting them to cross here because it was too far south. Lula May imagined the teams of police waiting for them in El Paso or Laredo – or maybe even as far north as Albuquerque – with their guns drawn. She had tried to assure herself: *There's still time. The custom guards will find something wrong with us. I know they will.* And then they passed the Brownsville turnstiles, where people crossing the bridge on foot were putting in coins. Then they were driving over the Rio Bravo bridge, and then they were on the other side. *Dear Jesus,* she prayed, *please help me.*

Clovis twisted the wheel west onto Highway 2, following the river to Reynosa and then Monterrey; he twisted them into tumbling sun, Miss Sugar miles behind them.

They arrived at the Monterrey market after the glaring fury of the noon sun and before the forgetful coolness of dusk. The market was a crush of elbows, hollering vendors, lanky dogs lapping in and out between the stalls, eating garbage off the pavement. Clovis bought tacos, which they ate while watching sun-burned tourists clad in white shorts and little white socks scuttle from stall to stall to test the weave of brightly coloured cloth; others limply rested in the shade on the low cement wall that circled the market. Everywhere the tourists went they left trails smelling of suntan lotion. In their dull, dingy work clothes Lula May and Clovis did not look like tourists, but Clovis said it was important that they did in a hurry. Above the stalls, long Mexican skirts hung from hooks and wires set up like clotheslines. Clovis pulled one down then another.

"What do you think?" he asked her. It was green, gauzy, and translucent when he held it to the sun.

She shook her head, feeding what remained of her taco to a flea-ridden dog.

"Well, what about this one?"

"Pink? Gawd, Clovis. I'm a redhead."

Clovis batted her hand away from the mutt's patchy head. "Choose something." Clovis's eyes were wide open, which made her think he must know the effect narrowing them on her had, sharpening them to green shards. "I don't know why you're being this way."

"Think about it," she said.

The restaurant smelled of hot grease, blue smoke rising in spires and clouding the overhead fan. Above the fryers was a hand-painted sign in Spanish she couldn't read. The plastic chairs and tables were covered entirely with Mexican beer labels.

Lula May twisted her paper napkin, tearing bits off the end into a pile on her lap, as she tried to gather together her thoughts on all the things that had happened since yesterday.

A breeze kicked in from Abasolo Street, where vendors and donkeys loaded with firewood crossed. The restaurant must have been a garage once; there was a big metal door at the front cranked open, leaving the insides exposed. There was no front wall to stop the dusty sidewalk scraps from swirling onto Lula May's toes, or any bird from flying in and around the metal girders. She remembered how humming-birds would fly into the windows of her family's farmhouse, breaking their necks as they hit the glass, falling in feathery heaps she would later find on the wooden porch. Sometimes the hummingbirds collided into the windows by accident, but at other times, on seeing their own reflections, they'd smash against the glass on the attack, mistaking themselves for the enemy.

Clovis held his beer to his forehead to cool down; the air in the restaurant was hotter than out on the street. Out past the restaurant's open front, past the dusty Mexican build-ings, was nothing but wide blue sky.

They arrived at the Motel El Capy late in the afternoon. Because the manager insisted they sign the guest book, Lula May registered them under fake names – her handwriting was better than Clovis's – and then they carried their bags, leather and new-smelling, to their room. They had bought them at the Monterrey market and filled them with new clothes she couldn't have imagined herself ever wearing before. Clovis had bought pants and belts, shawls and T-shirts, wooden birds, even postcards like a man actually on vacation.

There was a swimming pool at the back of a tiled hall, cement-circled and fenced in from the drought-stricken hills. Clovis sat in one of the sand-pocked metal deck chairs, slugging straight from a forty of tequila even though she had set a tray with lime, soda, and glasses by his feet before stretching herself out on a towel. Clouds came like a gift, wrapping sheets of coolness around the searing sun.

Clovis ignored the tray and took another drink from the bottle. "Did I tell you what it was that made me decide to rob that bank?" he said, circling his finger around the lip of the bottle. She turned his words into big bubbles, nothing but shape and sound, and let them float past the pool chairs and up over the fence. "That fire was the last straw. You started believing the worst then; that nothing was gonna come of the mine. And what you had to put up with in the meantime . . . It did something to me too, me and my big-assed ideas. See, justice is something everyone's got waiting for them, like in a big cosmic storehouse."

Justice? She could've laughed, knowing what she did. But she tried not to let herself think about Clovis's .38, or Miss Sugar on her knees. Lula May turned away so she wouldn't have to look at him wiping tequila off his chin with the heel of his hand. As she rolled over onto her stomach, she couldn't help but think how at that precise moment there was nothing she liked about him.

Lula May sat up and poured him a proper drink, even wedging a lime slice into the glass. She made him another drink. Then another. She made them bigger every time.

That night, while Clovis lay in bed alone in the motel room, continuing to drink, Lula May sat outside in the courtyard, gazing at the door to their room. She was watching a gecko on the white exterior wall to the left of the door, flicking its hungry tongue at the light hitched up to an iron wall peg, drawing moths that flittered on the brink of the gecko's reach. Moth after moth flying blind into that double-trap: the light, the gecko. At any point they could have flown away. But instead they kept flocking, closer and closer to the light, and closer to the gecko's mouth.

Miss Sugar had let herself be led from the truck on the road, through the bush, and then into the clearing.

Lula May and Clovis had started walking back to the truck when she glanced behind her. Miss Sugar was still standing there, in the middle of the clearing, like a plucked flower, unmoving and half-bent. Her eyes darted over the yuccas then shifted to the sky. She took two small steps, as if testing the air in front of her, and then stopped. Her eyes turned to Lula May, all wide-open and begging.

"Run, goddammit, run!" Lula May screamed. "Can't you see you're free?"

The night Clovis died Lula May blamed Miss Sugar for being weak, for allowing herself to be taken hostage. She blamed Clovis for driving them into Mexico, for making Lula May go get the truck, for robbing the City Trust on her account. She blamed Clovis for making her love him too much, for tying up Miss Sugar on his sweetgum bed, for what she saw after she'd come back with the truck and pushed aside the door of his shack. For how even after Lula May's eyes adjusted to the shadows and saw that his pants were undone and Miss Sugar was on her knees, she still loved him. Miss Sugar's face was wooden and her eyes were dead-looking, unblinking. Clovis had the most peculiar expression on his face, as if he couldn't decide whether to shout at Lula May or laugh. She closed the door quietly and sat outside the shack, chewing on her nails until he came and got her. She blamed him for her love, for how even at that moment she would've died for him.

The motel room was humid and the air felt like bath water against her skin. Clovis was tossing-and-turning drunk, moaning on the bed.

She got the bottle of Valium from the glove compartment of the truck and crushed a handful of them into a fine dust with the edge of the empty tequila bottle; then she added some water, opened his mouth, and poured the mixture over his tongue and down his throat. He was so drunk he didn't put up a fight. After a time his skin flushed and started to sweat; his eyelids fluttered. She kissed him, smoothing his hair away from his forehead.

She remembered his last words, languidly drifting over the nubby bedspread and out the window: "You've become so beautiful. Lu-la, lusc-ious Lu-la."

His face was wet and flecked with the green-and-orange patterns of the back-lit curtain, and then his jaw clenched.

She rocked back and forth on the bed by his feet, hugging her knees as he writhed on the tangled sheets. Once his stare remained fixed on the ceiling and his eyes stopped blinking, she peeled the sheets back and slipped between them like a lizard in a crevice, curling around his body. She unfolded his fingers one by one and ran them through her hair. She pressed his hands to her face, ran his callused fingers over the little bump on the bridge of her nose. She played with her breasts and put his fingers inside her: he would always be hers.

Afterward, she ran a bath and scrubbed herself until she was surrounded by islands of skin floating on the water. Her mother would be at home, sitting by the phone, clenching her hands out of worry, waiting for any news of Lula May. She can see the police knocking on her parents' door. Her father's flustered face as he holds the screen open with his shoulder. Her mother next to him, eyebrows raised, shaking her head, refusing to believe the story coming out of the officer's mouth is true. Lula May scrubbed until her skin was raw, but still she stayed in the bath long after the water had grown cold around her.

Before she left the motel, she counted the money and stuffed the stacks in her luggage, jacket, underwear, boots. Abandoning Clovis's pickup in the motel parking lot, Lula May caught a ride with a trucker into town and let him buy her breakfast.

At the Transporte del Norte bus station on Echeveria and Garza, a man in cut-off jean shorts with a fish knife in his belt loop was purchasing a ticket to Acapulco. He noticed Lula May staring at him, and smiled. He was wearing a baseball cap advertising a New Mexico insurance company. His hands were small, so unlike Clovis's, and his teeth reminded her of yucca flowers that belong to no one but the hills. Even as she returned his smile, she knew she could never love him, not in all the breaths of a lifetime.

FLOATING LIKE THE DEAD

C leaning his ear with a long stalk of grass, Ah Sing filled his wood stove with kindling. Outside, the alder leaves were fluttering in the trees, displaying their yellow undersides, which often meant rain. Ah Sing shivered, but did not light the fire; instead, he put a rough wool jacket over his cotton shirt. His room had no hooks, but all his clothing was tidily folded and stacked on the wooden stool in the corner by the door. On top of the clothes he laid a few bone-white sticks. Sun-bleached, lighter than the pine branches he had originally whittled down for his kite, the driftwood would make a good frame. He sneezed and shivered again. He had lost his upper incisor yesterday.

The nerves in Ah Sing's arms and legs had grown hard as jade; he was turning into a mountain, solidifying. His face resembled a palace statue. Smooth. Hairless. The skin so taut it looked varnished. He had lost his eyelashes and three-quarters of his eyebrows; lately, his ulcerated feet left tracks of blood on the wood floor. But he refused to wear the government-issue overshoes. His extremities felt no heat, no cold, no pain, anyway. In the next life he would be a mountain, the mountain he was now turning into, eternal and unyielding.

He had wept at the official diagnosis of leprosy.

"They sick but I not," Ah Sing would say in English to the doctors who accompanied the steamer *Alert* to the island and took flakes of skin from the backs of his hands. (Speaking English was masonry work, the words like bricks laid by hand; he spoke Cantonese with the other men on the colony, and the words flowed easily then, even when they had nothing to say.) When the doctors asked about his lost fingers, he explained, "Coal mine in Nanaimo. Frostbite." He had difficulty pronouncing the word and it came out sounding like "flossed bite." Grunting once or twice, he would pry an oyster off a stone with his remaining fingers and hold it up.

"You send away Ah Sing," he always said to the visiting doctors, "back to China."

Earlier today Ah Sing had fallen asleep on the beach next to his half-eaten lunch of sea urchins. Awoken by the sound of birds scavenging near his head, he had opened his eyes and was startled to see four black cormorants flying away. They reminded him of the cormorants he had felt sorry for when he was six years old and had laughed at by the age of nine, black birds circling the ancient uplifted seabeds in Chongwu Bay, catching fish they could taste but never swallow because of the white choke collars around their necks.

Three men left on D'Arcy Island now. They lived in the main building, in four cubicles set side by side, each with its own door opening out onto a verandah facing Cordova Bay. Ge Shou hadn't been right in the head since a tree fell on him, and he spent his nights in the woods singing. Gold Tooth, who had never told Ah Sing his real name, cried all day and then sat at the edge of the forest, dulled and deadened, refusing to move. He had a cough that possessed him like a malevolent spirit, wracking his body until he spat blood. He was the island's newest resident.

Gold Tooth had arrived at the colony three years ago with his bowler hat and a Swiss pocket watch on a chain. Slipping on patches of seagrass in leather shoes, over barnacle-covered stones still wet from the tide, refusing any attempts at help from the government official from Victoria. Ah Sing had laughed at his vanity, but the watch – the watch – was as round as an eye. He stared at it until he felt like he was staring into a thousand tiny suns.

When they had the energy, Ah Sing and Ge Shou said they would murder the filthy thief while he slept. But the daily chores sapped their passion – the harvesting of clams and mussels, the chopping of firewood, the collection of rain water from below the eaves or in the summer from the bog. Most days, when Ah Sing had finished his tasks, he would sit on the boulders that ringed the bay and watch the waves, pondering Buddha's question: *How does one stop a drop of water from ever drying out?*

Now, in his room, Ah Sing picked up his buck knife and eyed the driftwood he'd been gathering every time he walked the beach. He was searching for the most evenly balanced of sticks. He would carve carefully measured slits into which he would neatly wedge two smaller sticks. He would wrap the joints with sewing thread. He would cut a tail to look like phoenix wings, or find some cormorant feathers on the beach to stand in their place.

As shavings curled around his feet, he remembered how, as a child, he had believed the most ornate kites could talk to the spirits. The painted silk would deliver messages on behalf of the hands that held the slender thread. His thoughts were interrupted by the sound of something heavy being dragged across the wooden floor. He heard a sob. Another.

Gold Tooth was on the verandah, dappled light sifting through the fir trees and falling in shadows across his back. Though it was hard to tell which were shadows and which were stains, for Ah Sing could not remember when Gold Tooth had last taken off the silk suit he wore. Gold Tooth's face was flushed with terror and his eyes darted like birds in the trees, afraid of being caught.

"Take it easy. What are you doing with your bed?"

Gold Tooth shook off Ah Sing's hand the way a dog shakes off water. He tried to haul the cot through the doorway, but it got stuck. "I can't breathe," he said. "I can't breathe in there. The walls. They'll crush me if, if I go to sleep." He yanked at the bed again before stumbling backward.

"Do you want me to hold up the walls while you pull your bed outside?"

Gold Tooth stopped yanking.

Ah Sing climbed over the straw mattress and into the foul-smelling room. Ever since Gold Tooth had stopped taking care of himself, he'd left his door open for the racoons to come and go as they pleased, and now half-eaten plates of food lay scattered from one side to the other.

Ah Sing, his legs shoulder-width apart, spread his arms wide against the two walls and held them with his remaining fingers so they wouldn't crush Gold Tooth as he dislodged the bed from the doorway and wrestled it outside.

On the verandah, Gold Tooth nodded toward the forest then motioned to Ah Sing. "Pick up that end," he said.

The two men carried the wooden bed and straw mattress past roaming chickens and beyond the storage shed, where they kept the rice, sugar, flour, gardening tools, and coffins. They carried the bed beyond the withered vegetable garden. Past three graves, each marked with a pile of stones – the resting places of the men who had arrived with Ah Sing when the provincial government had left them on this island four years ago with a load of construction supplies. They carried it past the bog and into the forest. Ge Shou had been following them since they passed the garden.

"Do you have any pigs' feet for me?" Ge Shou asked.

Ah Sing shook his head.

"Can we fly your kite?"

"When it's ready, I promise."

"Washing Matilda, washing Matilda," Ge Shou sang, "who'll come a-washing Matilda with me?" He stopped and stretched his arms above his head. "Are you going swimming tonight, Sing, you going swimming in the ocean?"

"No, not tonight."

"Swimming, swimming." Ge Shou breaststroked the air. "Swimming in the ocean. I feel happy. Washing Matilda, you'll come a-washing Matilda with me?"

Ah Sing and Gold Tooth set the bed down in a clearing among the ferns and salal, where the ground was soft with pine needles. Through the trees they could see the ditch system that ran from the bog to the garden, where they had once grown potatoes, carrots, and onions; Ge Shou was playing among the lettuce that had gone to seed. Gold Tooth tumbled onto his bed, shivering, and immediately rolled onto his side as if in a deep sleep.

Ah Sing shook his shoulder.

"Go away."

After sitting near Gold Tooth for a time, Ah Sing came to a decision. He shuffled past the crops, which had spoiled before the men with their waning appetites had been able to eat them, and the pigs rooting in the waste. He nodded to Ge Shou, who sat among the pigs. He passed the plot of land they'd cleared of birch trees two years ago for an apple orchard.

Back in his cabin, Ah Sing filled his shoulder basket with a Hudson's Bay blanket, a cast-iron kettle, a wok, a grouse he had killed just that morning with his shotgun, a handful of onions, some mint leaves, a cupful of cooking oil in a canning jar, and some government-issue opium. Returning to Gold Tooth, he touched his shoulder again. Gold Tooth grunted.

Ah Sing spread the blanket over him; then he placed stones on the ground in a circle around some kindling and lit a fire with the matches in his pocket. He emptied his shoulder basket, picked up the kettle, and went to the woodshed, piling as much cedar into his basket as he could carry. The load weighed him down. He trod to the bog, sinking deep into the mud. He dipped his kettle, filling it with brown water. When he came back, Gold Tooth continued to ignore him, but Ah Sing didn't mind. He added more branches to the fire and set the kettle upon them.

A few minutes later, Gold Tooth said, "Why do you talk to me?"

Ah Sing shrugged. Before the disease had made his threats to beat up the other men laughable, Gold Tooth had hoarded the best rations, stashing second barrels of salt pork in his cubicle while the others looked on with vacant eyes. But Ah Sing, at fifty-two, had himself hit a woman; had fondled the flesh of his brother's wife; had ignored the unemployed after the smelters closed; had beaten a man when he was drunk while onlookers cheered. He sat cross-legged by the fire, poking the embers with a stick. He felt feverish, strange. Far away through the trees, he could hear Ge Shou singing.

Ah Sing poured the oil into the wok and dried the canning jar with the hem of his shirt. He dropped two mint leaves inside the jar. The mint grew wild near the bog, and Ah Sing would gather and then hang the sprigs from his cabin's ceiling. He poured the boiling water into the canning jar and stirred a gram of opium paste into the liquid. The steam rose and scented the air with mint. He wrapped a green maple leaf around the jar and passed it to Gold Tooth, but Gold Tooth pushed it away.

Ah Sing put the jar on the ground. He fussed over the flames, moving the kettle to make room for the wok, then busied himself with the onions and the grouse until the aroma rose into the air, overpowering the mint.

"I used to be a cook, you know," Ah Sing said. "I worked for Mr. and Mrs. Edward Price in Victoria."

"Shit work."

Ah Sing moved coals and added more kindling to adjust the heat. He rotated the wok and stirred its contents with a stick, testing the mixture frequently and inhaling its scent with his eyes closed.

Gold Tooth turned to him and snorted. "Look down. Your hand."

"Oh," Ah Sing said. "I've burned myself."

A patch of flesh two inches wide was stuck to the outside of the wok.

"No one will notice. Look at your face. Have you glanced in a mirror lately?"

When the food was ready, Ah Sing placed the wok down between them. Gold Tooth eyed the food with a rare appetite Ah Sing had not seen in the man in weeks. Ah Sing chewed in silence, watching Gold Tooth eat; rough skinned and fused together, the nubs of his fingers as Gold Tooth scooped the mixture into his mouth were as strange and beautiful as elephant hooves.

"It gets easier," Ah Sing said.

"I'm not a leper."

"No one wants to believe they are. I'll tell you something. I'm going to escape. I've got to go back to China. To my son and wife."

Gold Tooth gave a disgusted grunt. "Has anyone escaped before?"

Ah Sing didn't answer. He told Gold Tooth he'd heard that two New York lepers had been shipped in a crate by the CPR as far west as Prince Rupert, and he thought they'd been deported to China from there. "My son," Ah Sing said, changing the subject. "My son would be eighteen years old now. He was five the last time I saw him. It would be good if he could come to Gold Mountain. He would find work."

They sat looking at each other while dusk fell. Neither one said a word. Ah Sing cracked open grouse bones and sucked out the marrow. Gold Tooth lay on his back and smoked tobacco from the supply ship. The fire had turned to coals and the coals had turned to ash before Gold Tooth spoke.

"I used to get all the girls. Best one's name was Zao. I called her 'Zao,' *chirp,* because of the sound she made when we had sex. On hot nights she ran ice cubes up and down my spine, and on cold nights she tickled me with cotton balls. When I couldn't sleep, she massaged my feet while humming Strauss. She polished my shoes and every morning brought me my gambling spreadsheets. The way she penciled in her eyebrows. I'm going to give you a piece of advice. Only hit a woman when she needs it, and only with an open hand. You got to keep them in their place because they want it. You have to answer their questions for them; that's love."

"Did she turn you in?" Ah Sing asked.

"No!" Then after a moment he said, "They raided the Kwong Wo and Company Store; we were in the back, gambling."

It was pitch black now. Ah Sing drew a stick through the ashes. The bark caught an ember and he blew at the small flame. He threw on more kindling until the wood crackled. The only light came from the small campfire; its shadows highlighting the heavy ridges of Gold Tooth's overgrown brow.

"When I was a kid I found this bottle with a note inside," Gold Tooth continued. "It'd washed up from Taiwan," he said. "Funny thing is I don't remember what the letter said. It was a wide, fat bottle, like a medicine bottle. It was dull, scratched up by the rocks. I remember grabbing it and trying to open it while the older boys were gambling by the fishboats, and then it started to rain and I ran under an overturned dory. I tried to pry out the cork, but it was stuck fast. Then I tried to cut it out with a broken clam shell. I ended up smashing the neck off. I remember the bottle, but not the message. Strange, huh?"

Ah Sing drew his knees up to his chest. "Memory is a funny thing."

"I wonder what it said. Who knows? I don't remember."

Ah Sing didn't answer.

"I remember lots of other things. Swimming in the Zhu Jiang River. The ducks and geese. I ate lily roots. I loved water chestnuts and dates. Have you been to the hills of Guangxi? Limestone towers. I would visit my uncle and play in the fish ponds."

Gold Tooth turned on his side, away from Ah Sing, and curled up in the fetal position. Ah Sing's mother had turned on her side and died facing the wall. She had first lain in bed talking about her childhood, but as the sun rose, she turned inward and fell silent.

"In Canton the laundry waved like flags. We threw cats into the stinking canals. My parents were dead. I stole food from the people who lived on boats along the waterfront. I ran through the alleys and when I made the cut-throat sign people feared me. I grew up to be a Tong, never did any grunt work. Laundry, houseboy, gardener. Never did any of that. I was in extortion."

An hour or so later, Gold Tooth started to cry, softly, under his breath. He mumbled something inaudible.

"What?"

"Will you send my bones back to China?"

Ah Sing sat up.

"You know the worst thing about it?"

"What?"

"I never knew her real name."

"Who?"

"First it was the cotton balls, I couldn't feel them. Then I couldn't feel the suit against my skin. This is my best suit. My best suit."

"I called her Zao," he said. He started sobbing.

Ah Sing dozed in the forest to the sound of Gold Tooth's laboured breathing. The stretches between his exhalations grew longer, as if each breath was becoming too precious to release. A breath. Another. He clutched the life within him and refused to unleash it, greedily holding onto the air inside his lungs for ten seconds at a time, fifteen, twenty.

Ah Sing dreamed a man holding a roomful of rice in the palm of his hand was trying to make him swallow it all, and awoke choking. Gold Tooth's eyes appeared fixed on an immature bald eagle circling overhead, and in the dawn light he looked like he was still alive. Ah Sing rubbed his hands vigorously over his own cheeks. He closed Gold Tooth's eyelids and touched the man's chest. He felt along the body, found the Swiss pocket watch and slipped it into his own pocket. An object valuable enough to buy passage off the island, maybe even to pay the deportation costs back to China. Ah Sing couldn't see clearly and stumbled toward

the ocean, moving branches away from his face as he made
his way through the brush.

He ran to the beach, and raised the emergency flag on
the hill.

The Victoria Tug Company steamer *Alert* usually arrived
quarterly to deliver supplies: tea, dried fish, axes, razors,
handkerchiefs, and, in the last load, a looking glass. It was
surprising to see the tug so soon; often they would raise
the flag and no one would show up for weeks.

Ah Sing had fought to bury Gold Tooth in his silk suit, but
Ge Shou had slipped away with the jacket. So when the boat
came, Ah Sing was digging alone near the bog, past the vegetable garden, where the ground was soft, and far enough
away from Ah Sing's cabin that even a spirit as restless as
Gold Tooth's couldn't haunt him.

As the steamer cut through the chop, Ah Sing flung a last
shovel of soil onto the coffin he had dragged out of the storage shed. Then, brushing his hands together, he scrambled
down the gravelled slope to the shore, pebbles tumbling
away from the edges of his footsteps. He watched as a dory
loaded with supplies was lowered from the boat and rowed
toward the shore with two men aboard.

Ah Sing grabbed hold of the wooden dory, helping to pull
it onto the beach. A man with a red moustache that hid his
upper lip got out of it with the doctor.

The doctor straightened his back.

"Good, sir. Still strong, see?" Ah Sing said, lifting a
barrel from the bottom of the boat.

Ah Sing recounted what had happened the night before.

The doctor pulled a bag from the dory and withdrew a ledger of dates, names, and other notes. He looked down his spectacles.

"The one you call . . . Go Chou?"

"No, sir."

"Fong Wah Yuen."

Ah Sing shrugged. "We call him Gold Tooth. Not know his real name."

The doctor wrote something in his ledger and turned toward the main building.

When the doctor was halfway up the slope, Ah Sing tilted his head in the direction of a termite-filigreed log to indicate he wished a word with the other man, whom the doctor had introduced as a reporter. He was wearing a hat with feathers on the side, and his pants were cinched high upon his waist. He took two steps toward the log and stood, smoothing his hands over his thighs.

Ah Sing stepped over to the log and sat down. His mouth was dry. The man was smiling, but his gaze jumped from Ah Sing to a spot beyond his head, then back to Ah Sing, then to the doctor stumbling up the gravel slope. The man continued to stand.

Ah Sing cleared his throat. "I favour you . . . no, me . . . no, you favour me." The disease in his larynx made his voice no more than a loud whisper. "I, I have something." He stood up and pulled the Swiss watch from his pocket, where he had been clutching it so tightly that it was slick with sweat. He wiped it against the leg of his pants. He dangled it between them, letting it catch the sun.

"This is for you," Ah Sing said.

"Look at that." The man removed his hat and scratched his head, squinting at the shining metal.

"Nice, yes?"

The man nodded. "This is a nice island," he said, rubbing the back of his neck. He looked from the boulders that ringed one side of the bay to the mud flats on the other. He glanced at the doctor, who was talking to Ge Shou at the main building. "I hear you men hunt, and fish, too."

"You take."

"No." The man's moustache brushed his bottom lip when he spoke. "I don't think I should."

"No," Ah Sing nodded his head. "For you."

The man looked down at the watch.

"But is gift."

The man fingered his eyebrows.

"Gift," Ah Sing repeated. "A gift for you. Your wife?"

On the verandah of the cabin, Ge Shou danced, circling the doctor, his long black ponytail bouncing on his back.

A sudden gust of wind blew the reporter's hat off his head. It rolled a few feet, snagged on a log, then rolled away again with the next gust. The man chased after it, but Ah Sing bounded ahead, stopping the hat with his bare foot. Ah Sing dusted off the sand and shards of clamshell. He held the hat out toward the man.

"Oh. Well, then." The man inched his fingertips forward. "Thank you."

The man took his hat between his thumb and forefinger and walked to the dory. Leaning into the boat, he dropped the hat onto one of the seats. He grabbed a heavy sack. Ah Sing did the same. Sack after sack, barrel after barrel, crate after crate, the two men, Ah Sing and the reporter, worked in this way until they had unloaded the boat. When the man began rolling a barrel up the beach toward the slope, his shoes slapping on the gravel, Ah Sing rushed after him.

"Gift, you help me. Gift," he said, his throat tightening so he could not swallow. "Please, please, you take." He pushed out a laugh. It felt like choking on a ball of rice. "You remember Ah Sing to the CPR."

The man stopped, his eyes focused on Ah Sing for the first time, clear blue eyes the colour of frozen ponds in the spring when the ice cracks. Ah Sing was sure he heard the man sigh. The man shifted his weight from one foot to the other and rubbed his wiry eyebrows that shot straight up.

Ah Sing held the watch in his open palm. He imagined slapping it into the man's hand. The man would laugh and throw it over his shoulder; it would shatter into a thousand golden pieces.

"It *is* a beautiful timepiece," the reporter said.

"Yes, beautiful," Ah Sing answered. His throat was a bird's throat, filled with small stones.

"A gift, you take."

Ah Sing thought he saw the man quiver just a little. "Right, then. Thank you." Almost without touching it, he dropped the watch into his jacket pocket.

Then he said, "Look, man, look what I have here." He undid the buttons of his tweed jacket and fished around in the breast pocket of his blue shirt, the same colour as his eyes. "Here, look at this. This is a Kruger coin. All the way from the South African Republic."

Ah Sing raised what was left of his eyebrows.

"I've got some others at home, a pocketful, in fact. But they're rare, quite rare, in spite of that. You'd have to go all the way to the South African Republic; I came back with them after the Boer War." The man stopped and buffed the coin against his chest. "If you would take this as a sign of my appreciation."

Ah Sing stared at the coin. He felt an ache in the bottom of his stomach. It grew worse. He would vomit. He knew it. His legs tensed, waiting for the spasm. He imagined running. Running. The man would start chasing him. Would throw handfuls of Kruger coins. They would hit him on the back, handful after handful. Stinging, like golden hail. What a silly, infuriating man. Ah Sing could decorate his cabin. He could use them as sinkers when he fished.

Ah Sing held the coin between his thumb and forefinger. He spat on its tarnished surface.

The man widened his eyes.

"Superstition. It bring more money when spit. Bring good luck."

"Oh," the man said. He clapped his hands together. "Well, then."

Far from shore, the steamer bobbed in the chop. A crow cawed. The waves tumbled.

The man walked to the dory and Ah Sing followed. Reaching in, the man picked up his hat from where it lay. It was a green plaid cheese cutter with yellow and orange stripes. Under the leather strap at the back he had tucked some heron feathers, and for an instant Ah Sing was reminded of the ladies of Victoria who had worn hats adorned with enough feathers to drive certain birds to extinction. The wealthy of Victoria who had called men like Ah Sing their "Celestials." Romanticizing their roast duck, their porcelain figurines for sale in every Chinatown store, their opium pipes.

The man held his hat out to Ah Sing. "Do you like this hat?"

"It fine hat."

"Take it."

Ah Sing walked with the hat on his head and the coin in his pocket where the watch had been, counting his footsteps as he rolled a barrel up the slope. He fought against quick breaths, trying not to hyperventilate. He stacked the barrel in the storage shed next to the coffins and the axes.

He was walking toward the cabin, staring at his feet, when something hit his shoulder. He glanced up at the sky. A heron in the fir tree. He looked at the ground. Frog bones. And he noticed a drop of red blood that had fallen onto a green alder leaf.

In his cabin, he packed an empty burlap bag with his driftwood pieces, his buck knife, his cast-iron kettle, and his tin cup. He surveyed the room, the clothes folded on the stool by the door, the walls papered with the *Daily Colonist* and Chinese New Year's decorations, their glossy gold characters jumping off the red background. Then he went back to the beach.

He sat in the loose shale by the boulders. He dug for his buck knife in his bag. Waiting, he whittled eight sticks and two larger ones. He carved notches into the two big sticks and then he fitted in the small ones, tying them each in turn. If he finished in time, he could leave the kite for Ge Shou.

Leaning against a boulder, watching the ocean, Ah Sing

was reminded of his thirty-ninth year. With his back against the rock wall of Kwangtung and the South China Sea spread out wide before him – trapped by famines in Anhui across the border, and by the dirt and drought of Jing Gang on the eastern border with Hunan – he had paid a CPR labour broker and hopped a freighter bound for Canada. He smiled now, remembering. As the journey progressed, his excitement had been replaced by tense muscles. He had felt trapped, with no breath, no arms to fight; the mountains of black waves spanned for miles in all directions. How he had trembled on the deck! How he had been convinced the waves would swallow him, the same way Gold Tooth had trembled on the verandah as he hauled his bed outside, convinced the walls would crush him – solid walls that Ah Sing himself had built. And how, on the freighter, another man from Fujian had touched Ah Sing on the shoulder. The man had said, "There's nothing to be afraid of."

The sun shifted; the boulders cooled. In the distance he saw the reporter and the doctor. They were taking off their shoes and wading out to the dory.

"Hallo! Hallo!" Ah Sing yelled.

They nodded to him and waved.

He stood up. He threw his bag around his shoulder.

They plunged their oars into the water. They were rowing back to the *Alert* that pitched offshore. Ah Sing narrowed his eyes at the doctor and reporter and could feel the wind ripple across his bare neck.

He bent down and dropped his knife back into his bag. He could hear the waves, and Ge Shou singing closer to shore. He touched the coin in his pocket. His jaw tightened.

He undressed so quickly his shirt got caught on his ears. He pulled down his pants and dropped his wool shirt onto the rock next to his bag.

"Hallo! Hallo!"

He dove. His breath froze inside his lungs, and his limbs seized up: he was a stone, armless and legless. He began to sink, watching the bubbles rising past his face.

Fear made a body heavy; fear made a person sink and drown. Dead bodies floated because all the fear was gone. Once, a leper had tried to swim toward the lights of Cordova Bay. His body had floated with the grace of a lotus flower back to the gravel slope. Then Ah Sing and Ge Shou had buried him, silently, beyond the goldenrods. If only he had let the water flow through him as if he were made of it, he could have floated to freedom. Another leper had once escaped D'Arcy Island by swallowing a vial of poison. He swallowed it on board the steamer, had died before even arriving at the colony.

Ah Sing thought he would never stop sinking, but then his arms and legs sprang to life. He kicked as fast as he could while whitecaps crashed around his ears. The doctor and the reporter were not waiting. He slapped the water. He cried into the wind, his eyes open against the salt and the horrifying green.

The seagulls laughed. Ah Sing sputtered, yet the two men ignored him and boarded the steamer. His breath felt scant and thread-like in his lungs. His ears rang; his head thudded.

He plunged his head under. When he surfaced, he squinted at Ge Shou standing on the rocky outcrop of beach. Ge Shou had picked up his clothes and was waving them, flag-like. Then he reached for the kite, but stopped short of picking it up.

Ah Sing swam back to shore and clung to a rock. Ge Shou looked down in silence. Ah Sing breathed deeply, filling his nostrils with salt air and water droplets that burned. He wiped his eyes with the back of his hand. Water remained on his lashless lids and formed prisms, through which he looked at the setting sun. Above them, oystercatchers circled and screeched.

Ge Shou lowered his hand to help Ah Sing onto the boulder. Ah Sing shook his head. He spat over his shoulder and then heaved his body out, panting as he clambered up. There he hunched forward and held himself.

After a while, he stood and picked up the hat from the rock; he put his fist in the centre and spun the hat a few times. Holding it aloft, he pulled out the heron feathers. Maybe he could use them to decorate his kite. Then he put the hat down.

He reached for the coin and put it in his mouth. It tasted like oak. His tongue moved it from one side of his mouth to the other and warmed the metal. He spat the coin back out, into his hand, and hurled it toward the ocean. It glinted in the air. When it hit the water, it skimmed the surface like a cormorant before sinking into the grey-green waves.

A breeze dimpled the ocean. Ah Sing picked up the kite frame and offered it to Ge Shou. Ge Shou rubbed his forehead.

"Don't be scared, Ge Shou."

Ge Shou hopped from foot to foot, holding the kite.

"Don't cry, Ge Shou."

Ah Sing put his arm around Ge Shou's shoulder and stroked him up and down. He could feel the warmth of the man's flesh through the damp cotton of his shirt. Ah Sing's arm was covered in goose pimples. Ge Shou's black braid tickled his armpit.

"There's nothing to be afraid of," he said to Ge Shou. "Do you want to help me fly the kite?"

When he was a boy, Ah Sing's bed had been a strong rush mat and he had slept on it with his four brothers and sisters, his parents, and their parents, by the great mouth of the Yangtze River where it emptied into the East China Sea.

The sea touched everything with lapping hands, probing fingers, reaching across countries and exploring fjords with whales, bays of volcanic rock, and ancient crevasses. A single drop could eventually circumnavigate the globe.

As a boy, he would float in the warm waters of Chongwu Bay until he felt his body liquefying, his loose limbs pulled by small currents and pushed by gentle swells. He would float as if he were dead while the sun burned his back. Then he grew and fished with the older boys. He went to work in the tin mines of Malaysia. He went to the plantations of Borneo. He forgot how to turn into the sea.

The water dripping from his body had formed a puddle at his feet. Ah Sing shook the remaining drops from his limbs and stood on one leg to dry the bottom of his feet with his shirt. Then he used his shirt to towel the top of his head. He stepped into his pants. He pulled his shirt over his head and the hair that was still wet dripped water down his back. The fabric of the shirt clung to his skin.

The warmth slowly returned to his body, but the back of his head still ached with cold. He looked out over the water.

"Hey Ge Shou, here's a riddle for you: *How does one stop a drop of water from ever drying out?*"

"A riddle." Ge Shou clapped. "I love riddles."

———

"Ah, this is the life," Chinchu says. "The sun, the waves, and licking opium off the hand of a beautiful woman."

Even after all these months in Zipolite with Chinchu, to her ears the rhythm of the Spanish language still sounds like a machine gun — *rat-tat-tat* — hard consonants battering the palate.

She pulls her hand away from him and begins to wrap in plastic the raw opium she's cut into grams with the knife on her nail clippers and rolled into balls, tying the packages closed with the strands of sewing thread gripped between her teeth. She has yet to devise a way to divide the black paste without staining her fingers with a sticky residue, defiling her hands. When she is finished, she lets Chinchu take her fingers into his mouth again.

Outside their *cabaña*, another column of buyers is already

advancing through the sandy yard. Closing the door, pretending she's out, is futile. The addicts will thump the bamboo
slats, call out like tireless automatons, rattling the bicycle
chain that keeps the door locked.

She came to Mexico because she wanted to volunteer in
an orphanage in the Chiapas mountains. She had imagined
saucer-eyed children clinging to her skirt hems while she
chanted the leftist slogans of the Popular Revolutionary
Army. But then she met Chinchu, and instead she finds herself greeting an endless wave of users at her door, some who
come to buy, others to trade useless items – ridiculous
winter coats, stolen watches, walkmans with broken head-
phones. It is the price she pays for doing business in this
town, where she is a foreigner and an object of curiosity.
Through the open door, she watches a trio of addicts
approach in whirls of kicked-up sand.

"Done," she says to Chinchu, nodding at the opium balls.
"Your turn to take care of this group."

"*Cómo quieras,*" he says, but she is already out the door.
His words of easy compliance dissolve in the crashing waves
of the Pacific, which she can see from the courtyard, changing from green to grey, like a cat's eye.

In Roca Blanca, the neighbourhood where they live, their
cabaña is one of four circling the central courtyard. In the
hut to the left lives a fifteen-year-old mother whose six-
month-old baby cries half the night. The drunk in the hut to
the right weeps inexplicably whenever he sees the word
February on a calendar or in a newspaper. A dirt alley sepa-
rates them from another complex, where a Zapotec family
with dengue-fever-ridden children live. She hates Roca

Blanca, but stays for Chinchu. To respectable Zipolite citizens, Roca Blanca's reputation for immorality is matched only by its violence and the scandalous garbage heaps that line the junction of the alley and street, where someone has hung a sign that says: *Rincón del Paraíso*. Paradise Corner.

Flies buzz around the seatless toilet bowl that is in full view of the courtyard and only partially shielded from the busy alley by a few bougainvillea bushes and a low cement wall. Sometimes she walks two blocks to La Choza restaurant for the luxury of a bathroom door.

Most days, she unwinds by swimming the waves, though not always when the water is safest; not during siesta, when the beach is empty and the water is calm, nor at dusk when the ocean quiets its tumbling crests. The waves crash too dangerously for her to swim at dawn, and at midday they are worse still. When she finally dives in, the current pushes and pulls and tugs at her like a mouth. The waves swell at a breakneck pace, then crash down upon her, pounding her limbs, spinning her as if she were seaweed, leaving her dizzy and incapable of propulsion.

After her swim, she goes to the Cinco de Mayo market. But today, her nerves are rattled, her whole body on edge. For weeks now Chinchu has been telling her that when Semana Santa comes the police will swoop down on the town, and unlucky dealers will find even their wrist watches confiscated; yet still she and Chinchu persist in their routines, as if believing they are protected by some kind of magic and immune to arrest. To forget her worries, she drinks on the stone steps of the church, draining the mescal bottle quickly before it has a chance to sweat its coolness all over her hand.

The women at the market tip an invisible flask and laugh. They've nicknamed her the *güera*, "fair-haired one," even though her hair is dark. Squatting behind mountains of plantain and dried fish, the market women call all the tourists, light skinned or not, *güera*, although they don't mean badly by it. She tries to pretend she's Mexican and dresses like a local in A-line skirts and plastic sandals. She even brags that she is from D.F., Mexico City, when customers ask what part of the country she's from, because she knows her accent won't give her away unless she speaks for too long.

She sells to tourists, but avoids getting to know them; they remind her of sheep that graze in a meadow until the grass is all eaten up. For them, Mexico is a photo opportunity, there for their viewing pleasure, like the postcards they buy of crumbling ruins and colonial buildings in elegant decay, mariachi bands and fire eaters, barefoot children and Zapatistas toting machine guns. She's seen tourists in the market handing out souvenir pennies from home with all the benevolence of monks. Sometimes they hand out pencils made in China that the children turn around and sell. An American tourist wearing a Tilley hat buys a bottle of cold beer for a Oaxacan construction worker pouring concrete. "*Gringo,*" the workman says as he drinks, smiling, raising his bottle to the man who grins back, oblivious to his own arrogance. But the locals are just as alien to her as the tourists; even if they weren't living in Spanish, hating in Spanish, or yelling this way at their dogs, the way they live would still feel foreign to her. With Chinchu at her side, however, she likes to think her foreignness fades away.

Today, the *campesinos* of the mountains are once again pro-
testing at the town plaza near the Palacio Municipal, handing
out pamphlets on indigenous rights and land reforms and
blocking the traffic on Calle Trujano. She wishes she was the
kind of person willing to fight in a land where expectations die
daily like the litters of puppies abandoned on street corners
all over Mexico's poorest neighbourhoods. Listening to their
impassioned speeches, blow-horned from a turned-over
orange crate, she brings the mescal bottle to her lips instead.

She knows she is malingering. Still she consumes whatever crosses her path, gorging herself like someone used to
starving. This is how you create memories, she tells herself,
until she feels sickened by all the pleasure. Chinchu's voice
rings in her ear. "Semana Santa is coming. No one's luck
lasts forever."

Every night at eleven she stuffs a matchbox full with opium
and goes to La Puesta nightclub, the most modern club in
Zipolite, with corresponding prices. She keeps her eyes on
the Spanish-stunted tourists who waver at the bar while
they wait for their change, smiling like actors who have forgotten their lines, but the bartender does a good business
not returning their money. Eventually, the cheated customers shuffle away into corners, clutching their drinks, and
examining the contents of their glass, trying to hide the
embarrassment of being swindled, the anger of having no
language with which to protest.

This is when she makes her approach and chats them up
in one of four languages, cautioning them to pay with exact
change the rest of the night, selling them her friendship and

then her opium. For many of the tourists – neo-hippies, international backpackers on a shoestring budget – the main attraction in Zipolite is the party. Most of the bars are open till dawn, and when the sun is on the horizon, she sometimes sees the tourists as they leave the bar, blind drunk and stumbling through the sand, so different from when they first arrived in town. Then, they were like children in a candy store, awestruck by possibility, reluctant to choose anything for fear of making the wrong choice. But the longer they stay, the more they devour everything as a solution.

Chinchu sings and plays guitar at a tourist restaurant called La Choza. Sometimes she watches him from the back of the bar, standing by the rough posts open to the breeze and the crashing roar of the ocean. She watches him perform; watches tanned European women cross and uncross their legs for him. She and Chinchu have never claimed sole rights to each other's bodies: it was part of what attracted her to him, his willingness to give her amnesty to pursue new conquests just as he did, even as he crooned the love songs for which Mexico was famous.

She had left the life of an environmental activist behind in Vancouver and had arrived in Mexico City eager for a fresh start. Then she'd been groped on the subway. On a bus bound for Puerto Escondido on the coast, she had stared out the window, feeling hopeful once again. Bandy cactus spread their limbs as if begging for rain, and as the bus neared the coast the hills became as lush as mango ripening in the hot sun. By the third morning she had arrived in Zipolite, the ocean tumbling before her, begging her to dip her toes in. At La Choza, French girls sat around a table, their backs audaciously arched, their cigarettes elegant at the end of limp wrists. They sat with men whose tanned shoulders sweated as their hands pounded furiously over resounding djembes. Other travellers smoked joints and gazed at her, lizard-eyed, as she entered with her backpack.

She noticed Chinchu right away. He was an Aztec god, his carved muscles like those ancient statues she'd seen long ago in the Museo Nacional. She walked toward his table and set her pack down on the ground. His guitar was leaning against his thigh.

"You have crazy eyes," he said in heavily accented English.

She reached between his legs and strummed the guitar. "I've been on a bus for days. I haven't slept well."

"To get to Zipolite as fast as you can?"

"I'm leaving in two days."

"No, you will grow roots and get stuck here like the coconut tree."

"I have the address of an orphanage in Chiapas," she said, and on some impulse, she touched his thigh. And still his voice, lingering in her ear, challenged her to defy his prediction.

Now, six months later, there is still something about him that makes her want to swallow him whole, make him belong to her. But tonight her appetite pulls her in another direction, away from him and toward the endless belt of thatch huts, bars, and restaurants that line the beach. She's looking for someone new, someone who will lash out at her with a hidden strength.

She scans the crowds in a rainbow of beach wear before asking a tourist eating corn on the cob with mayonnaise if he wants to buy some opium. When he grins at her, kernels of corn fall from his mouth and down the front of his mesh tank top. "I might buy some." He winks. "But only if you'll do some with me."

He has pink zinc ointment on his nose and short fingers like sausage ends. He's not her type at all, and she's not willing to play this game with him tonight.

"A hundred pesos," she says, asking for twice what she often charges the men she likes.

"Oh, really," he says. "Someone else was selling it for cheaper." His breath smells like garlic.

"Take it or leave it." But she doesn't wait for an answer. She gets up and leaves the restaurant. She walks along the beach before she visits another bar and passes a pack of dogs that wander through the streets, belonging to no one but calling everywhere home.

Every two weeks she goes to the mountains alone to rescore, having convinced Chinchu that someone needs to stay behind on the beach to look after their customers while she makes the fourteen-hour journey north to the Teotitlán District by bus. The opium her friend Dashon sells her is cultivated from the poppies he grows in a hidden field a short distance from his shack, which he hand-built from red clay and roble branches. From where the bus drops her off on the highway, his property is a half an hour's walk up steep, winding trails, and a one-hour hike away from the nearest town of Huaulta de Jiménez, where she stays with Chinchu's uncle. Dashon calls these highlands where he lives with his family *tejao*, the Mazatec word for "eagle's nest." It is something she's

reminded of whenever she stands at the edge of the mountain, six thousand feet above sea level, where she can see
everything, and even look down on the clouds.

Dashon's daughter, Juana, is nine years old; she has
wide red cheeks and eyes sharp as jet shards. Juana "irons"
her dresses by smoothing them out between the floor and
her straw petate where she sleeps so her weight will press
out the wrinkles. She sleeps in the same shack as her father,
mother, her brother Miguel, and her grandmother.

If Juana was her daughter, she would to take her out for
ice cream every day. She remembers with a physical ache of
happiness her last visit, when she and Juana had run along
the steep slopes covered in pine needles behind the shack
and over the white stones of dry riverbeds, playing hide and
seek in the trails that snaked through the ragged hillside.
When Juana's grandmother had rustled through the oak and
seen her, fallen on her rear end and laughing, she had
clucked dismissively, as though deriding her for being a
childish outsider who had lost her way. She had wanted to
say she had been born with a bad sense of direction to make
the grandmother laugh, but the old woman spoke only
Mazatec, and such a comment would have only revealed how
lost she was most of the time.

Now her eyes are watering as she watches Dashon's wife
prepare soupy beans and strips of deer meat over a cooking
fire, the acrid smoke hanging in thick screens, blackening
the walls. She knows this woman only as "Dashon's wife,"
and she is too intimidated by the way the woman reaches
into the fire, seemingly moving the coals with her bare
hands, to feel she deserves to know her name.

Juana and Miguel bring her their battered homework books. They have never seen the ocean so she draws them pictures of the strangest sea creatures she can imagine: eels, manta rays, and jellyfish.

Miguel is always the one with the questions: "Why are only some parts of the ocean wavy? Is a current also a monster? Would a shark eat your goats if you weren't paying attention?" Juana just giggles and twirls a strand of hair in her mouth.

After supper she sits outside, where Dashon joins her, smoking a pipe. Once again she invites him to bring his family down to the beach, for a vacation, the way she does every time she visits. "Maybe your children would like to see the ocean for themselves?"

He nods slowly, thoughtfully, as if it is a decision not to be taken lightly. "Yes," he says, finally. "This is a good idea."

But she knows the truth is that he says only what he thinks she wants to hear, whatever that may be. He will never bring his family to visit her. And she'll never be Mazatec. Not even Mexican. *Güera.* She would always be the *güera,* even when no one says the word.

Miguel and Juana cajole her into playing a while longer in the trails behind the shack before bed, their bodies casting moonlight shadows on the furrowed ground. Juana's plastic shoes slip off her feet, but even so she remains as sure footed as the goats that she leads daily to the river so they can drink. Miguel runs into the house and lights a stick with a flame from his mother's dying cooking fire, now almost entirely reduced to embers. He torches one of the prickle bushes that riddle the fields and are as flammable as any kindling, and under the light of the moon and the dancing flames, he plays his favourite game. "Come closer to the fire, women," he says, "it will protect you from the coyotes. Now, wait here while I shoot us a deer for dinner." Then he rushes into the blue darkness with his toy rifle. As they sit in front of the fire, waiting for him to return, Juana asks, "What colour is a jellyfish?"

"It has no colour. It's like a raindrop."

"Can you bring me back one? The next time you come?"

"No, *nena*. You don't want a jellyfish. It can't live here, not without the ocean."

"*Mande?*"

"Dried jellyfish are ugly. How about a necklace made of shells?"

"I don't understand."

"If I brought you one it would have changed into something different by the time it got here. It would be hard and shrivelled."

Juana pauses. "My grandmother has never left these mountains, either."

"But you'd like to see the ocean?"

Juana eyes her and then looks away, suddenly coy. "That's a silly question." She knits her arms around her chest. "Do you know that the lake here has piranhas in it?" Then she starts laughing and making snapping motions with her hands.

It's almost midnight by the time she finally stands up and prepares to walk back to Huautla. Dashon shakes his head. "It's too late tonight." He tells her there's no need for her to return to Chinchu's uncle's house, and unexpectedly he begins rearranging sacks, moving bowls and pans, sweeping the kitchen with a corn broom.

"What are you doing?"

"He's clearing the kitchen so you can sleep there," Juana says, grinning.

Dashon has never invited her to stay with his family before. Perhaps now they'll ask her again — invite her to visit them more often, even. She could look after Juana and Miguel while their parents work. She could teach them how to play Twister. She could lead the goats to the river while they play. She would have so much to do she'd never be lonely. And then at bedtime, she'd tuck them in and tell them stories: Haida myths, Coast Salish legends.

"Hey," she says to Juana. "We can tell each other stories until we fall asleep."

Juana and her father exchange words in Mazatec. The smile falls from Juana's face. "I have to sleep outside," she says.

"Why?"

Juana looks at her feet. "So you have enough room."

She doesn't even look at Dashon. She sees a flat clearing in the middle of the courtyard by a mound of corns. "Stop tidying up," she says to Dashon. "I'd rather sleep over there."

"Outside?" Juana says.

"You'll be eaten by wolves," Miguel says.

She picks up her backpack and heaves it across the courtyard, toward the corn, away from them. "I like wolves," she yells over her shoulder. Dashon throws his hands up with a look of parental confusion. Let them think she is crazy.

Her muscles tense with the anger and helplessness of a child as she watches Dashon gather wood and build her a campfire. Even the blanket the grandmother brings out and puts around her shoulders does not stop her body from shivering, though more from sadness than from the cold. She sits on the ground and begins to cry, but then the old woman snaps her fingers at her and, before disappearing into the shack, shakes her head at the foolishness of the outsider once again.

*

Chinchu's ponytail hangs down his back like a snake. Her own hair is not silky like his; she has to struggle with it every day, pick it free of knots. But she can run her fingers through his hair for hours, braiding it, until in annoyance he shakes his head free.

She feels safe when he lifts her in his arms and places her like a doll in his lap; his arms are brown and carved the way a river carves through stone. She lightly fingers his tattoos and asks for the story behind each one as she traces them up his arm: depictions of Chaac, the Maya rain god, who saved crops for the ransom of virgins; other ancient Maya symbols; sea creatures in honour of the ocean he loves. His shoulders swim with fish, sharks, and octopus that flick up and around his bronzed back.

"Will you marry me?" Chinchu asks her in jest, not for the first time.

But today, for the first time, she doesn't answer "Maybe on Thursday" or "On Tuesday." Instead, she says, "You already have a wife. And two kids in Veracruz. You haven't seen them in a year."

"Ah, yes. It would never work between us anyway," he says.

"Why not?"

"The language would get in the way."

She likes that Spanish sets the rules of engagement, that their arguments are curbed by her simple vocabulary. She doesn't have the words to tell him "I love you"; they don't exist for her in Spanish. Yet they can dance the salsa as if connected at the hip, breezing through drunken tourists, unaffected by obstacles. And so they continue on in the way they always have.

She steps toward him, suddenly nervous, and slips her hand around his slim waist and down his narrow hips. Suddenly he bites her lip and then kisses her on both cheeks. Then he laughs, as if surprised at himself. And all she can think is, "This is how it will always be with me and Chinchu."

His hands are thick and callused, strong as knots. They astonish her with their lithe, sinewy strength. Kneading her flesh, he can sometimes console her. But even as the sweat of her body mingles with his, she feels a surge of boredom begin to surface, rising fast.

Every now and then, when she is swimming in the ocean to get away from it all, she can almost see herself settled in the world, happy and alone. Then the waves continue to tumble and her body begins to ache, her heat drained by a cold current she hadn't noticed before that leaves her shivering.

The ocean never stops moving. Left to itself, the ocean is restless, as turbulent as it is deep. She used to believe there was no better cure for her ills than movement – the silver bullet for indisposition. Now, just watching the rolling waves and the people scattering then gathering again on the beach makes her sick with the sureness of it all. If the world stopped spinning, would the sea follow?

But the waves continue to fall forward and backward simultaneously, the undertow pulling away from the shore even as the white caps push forward, crashing onto the beach. And this display of warring desires reminds her again of what she'd rather not think about.

She's added to the Spanish she learned in first-year university. Spanish, French, German: she can make a go in all of them now. The thatch bars still twinkle as tantalizingly as eyes, promising more than they can give, and the beach hugs the bay like a pink pair of arms. But she's been here too long. She should move on.

The door to their *cabaña* is open. As soon as she enters she feels weak, not because Chinchu is in the hammock with a peroxide blond, whispering in Spanish to each other words she doesn't understand. Not because the woman is wearing a Che Guevara T-shirt over a wet bikini top, the water soaking through the thin fabric and outlining the shape of her breasts. She swallows hard because it's not these things at all. He is feeding the woman the rest of his *tamal,* sliding it piece by piece into her mouth.

She throws her beach towel on the floor. "By the way, how were sales?"

The woman's laugh sounds like a freight train screeching to a halt. "You es-speak Spanish good," she says in English, loudly, slowly, as though speaking to the deaf.

"*Mi amor,*" Chinchu says, stretching open his arms, his eyes glazed. "You want to relax with us a little? Come smoke a joint with us."

She turns her back to them, retrieves her opium from the dresser, and spreads the nail clippers, the plastic wrap, and the sewing thread out on the table. Chinchu starts to tell a familiar joke, how the American tourist walks into a restaurant . . .

"Only some Americans are funny," the *güera* says. "You can't make jokes about all of them." From the corner of her eye, she watches as the woman hits Chinchu on the shoulder and rolls onto her side, laughing.

Even after the woman leaves, she refuses to speak to Chinchu.

"I can't help you," he says, "if you don't tell me what's wrong."

Chinchu spends the next several nights with her in their single bed, until one night she tells him, "The bed's too small for both of us. I can't sleep." When he doesn't come home, she drinks until she can no longer stand and then tips onto the bed, unaware of her limbs, the bamboo shack diminished to one spinning corner, one bare light bulb, the remnants of her focus. In her drunken aggression she annexes every square inch of space, spreading like a bloodstain.

Sometimes she wakes up on the floor, or crying out in her sleep. Sometimes she goes to La Puesta and doesn't make it home, passing out in the courtyard instead. When she kicks and attacks in her stupor, it's all Chinchu can do to remove the money and opium from her bra so she will not get robbed.

She wakes one night to find him sitting ten feet away in the sand, his back against the trunk of a coconut tree, keeping watch.

"I don't need you to keep an eye on me," she hisses.

On the nights she does not fight him, he picks her up and carries her over his shoulder back inside.

Sometimes she tries to imagine a life with someone who has captured her heart. What that would be like — soapy palms touching as they wash the dishes, swinging side by side in a hammock, bickering then making up, buying plantain together at the Cinco de Mayo market — all the tedious elements of domesticity charged by real love. She pretends those arms can hold her. She wishes on it, the way someone who is dying might suddenly believe in God.

By the time the *güera* has finished packing up the opium she will smuggle down to the beach, it is dusk, thick and heavy. Beside her, Juana sighs, squats on her haunches, and blows a strand of black hair out of her eyes. As Dashon's daughter stares up at the stars, she wonders if the girl too is remembering how the sky looked on her last visit, burnished with moonlight, the mountain air so cold.

Dashon's wife makes hot chocolate, stirring the water in an iron pot over an open flame fed with corn husks. A breeze blows across the courtyard and the flames rise a little higher.

The *güera* takes a breath as if to speak. She wants to tell Dashon she's sorry for the way she acted on her last visit, but she can't. All day, as they sliced poppy heads open with razor blades so the opium could flow out, their exchanges were strained. When she cut her finger, she had tried to hide the bleeding. Then, without meeting her eyes, Dashon had grabbed her hand and wrapped her finger in a rag.

Dashon drinks from a tin cup; when he's done, he sets the cup down next to Juana's Barbie doll, on the stump of a dead tree, and picks up his backpack. "I'll be back in the morning," he tells everyone.

"Where are you going?" the *güera* asks.

"I'm going hunting," he says. He's never gone hunting during any of her previous visits.

"I'll come hunting with you," she says, knowing full well that in their culture women don't hunt deer with the men. But she's not Mazatec, so why play by their rules?

"No, I'll walk you to where the bus leaves."

Dashon's wife asks a question, and as Dashon responds to her in Mazatec, the stresses of his words sound like a plea. Dashon's wife doesn't look at the *güera*, but shrugs in an exasperated way.

"I'm Canadian," she hears herself explain to Dashon's wife, cringing at how silly it sounds even though she knows the woman speaks no Spanish. "I used to bushwhack for an environmental group," she continues, making the motion of cutting through brush with a machete. "I worked build-ing trails. We went up and down mountains. The hills were so steep we needed climbing ropes." She turns to Dashon. "I *can* keep up with you."

The children look at each other and laugh—loudly at first, then more hesitantly, waiting to see what the other will do next. The children translate what the *güera* has said to their mother. After a terrible pause, Dashon laughs, too.

Dashon's wife interrupts the laughter and says something to Dashon, who shakes his head. The sound of their language is soft, not like Spanish, and reminds her of the way the Mazatecs shake hands, not grasping, but palms kissing, slipping past each other, like silk.

Then Dashon's wife turns around and disappears into the shack. As soon as his wife is out of sight, Dashon stares disapprovingly at the *güera's* sheer, flowing skirt. She grabs the front of her skirt and knots it, so that when she is done the hem hangs above her knees. "Better?"

When Dashon's wife reemerges from the shack, she is holding a pair of Dashon's wool pants and smiling at her for the first time. This unexpected gesture from a woman whose name the *güera* has never known makes her throat constrict with pride, her eyes grow wet. "*Gracias.*" Moonlight paints a shadow picture of their hands touching as the pants are exchanged.

She puts the pants on underneath her skirt. The wool scratches her skin, and she has to roll the pants down at the waist to stop them from slipping over her hips. "Well? How do I look?"

Dashon eyes her up and down.

Miguel shoots the stars with an air rifle. "*Pow-pow, pow-pow.* So I can come hunting too, now?" He grins at his father, who tsks sharply and says, "Go help your sister."

Dashon and the *güera* stare each other down until the children return.

"Fried eggs and rolls, some meat . . ." The children list off the food they've packed in the cloth bundle. Then, as soon as Dashon has tossed her the sack, he starts off toward the trees.

Dashon tells her that flashlights will scare the deer, so for the first half hour, although he is often too far ahead for her to see, she keeps pace by following the sound of his footfalls in the dark. He's trying to lose her. It's not until she falls again that she hears him breathing hard. He, too, is exhausted.

By the time they come to a savannah where the brush is knee-deep, he has slowed his pace enough that she is walking behind him. "I wonder what the tourists at the beach would pay for a guided tour of these mountains," she says. Dashon's machete makes a clean sound as it slices through spiny bushes and brushwood, peeling back the forest's protective skin with one clean swipe.

"What do you think?" she continues. "You could take them on hikes. I could find a lot of people who'd want to see this side of Mexico."

She imagines living in the mountains among the red earth and corn fields with Juana two weeks of the month. She could rent a little place in Huautla de Jiménez. When she wasn't guiding tourists through the lawless mountain passes, maybe she and Juana could wander through the market in Huautla, examining bolts of cloth and draping the fabric over their shoulders, envisioning the dresses they would sew. Maybe she could buy a truck to convert into a tour bus and find groups of travellers wearing designer sandals who would pay her in American dollars for nature hikes through Oaxaca. With the profits she earns she could buy blankets for Juana's family, one for every room in their house, a new propane stove, a year's supply of light bulbs, and crates full of the mangoes that only grow wild on the tropical coast. Though the thought of Juana's mountains infiltrated by bug-repellent-scented tourists leaving cross-trainer tread marks in the dirt makes her uneasy, it would be her chance to invent a new life for herself.

"If I brought the tourists up," she says to Dashon again, "you could take them on hikes. What do you think?"

Dashon removes his hat and scratches his head as she waits for his response, his face masking any clue about how he really feels. Then, in the moonlight, she sees him smile to himself, and with the tone of a man accustomed to authority he says, "This is a good idea."

She follows Dashon in the dark, trotting behind him as quietly as possible, struggling to keep up with him as he ducks around fallen branches and over the stumps of dead oaks. Suddenly, he throws his hand palm out, brakes the rushing ground.

The trees are gripped in shadows. She imagines she sees something, registering movement in every rustling pine. Then the moon untangles itself from the branches and clouds above them and illuminates the earth. At once shifting shapes are pinned down. Even the air, inert and insubstantial, seems to crystallize in her nostrils.

A deer quivers, its white tail beating back and forth, steady as a pendulum.

She takes aim. Curls her finger around the cold trigger.

There is a moment of exhilaration as the rifle butt kicks her shoulder backward and she has to fight to keep her footing. Then the deer falls.

Her body alone understands what she has done: her shoulder is throbbing; her feet, numb as she walks with Dashon to where the deer has collapsed on its side. It opens and closes its mouth.

Dashon, shocked and pleased, chatters about a way for them to haul the deer home. "*Hazme un favor?* Can you hold one of the legs for me?"

She cannot pull her eyes away from the mouth. The hike must have taken more out of her than she realized because she can't catch her breath.

Dashon empties his pack and looks up at her as she holds an arm out against an oak tree to steady herself. He's waiting for her to help him field dress the carcass, and suddenly she wonders what the deer's ankle might feel like in her hand – slender, dying – but she can't do it. She can't move. Her body is frozen against the tree's trunk and her hands are clenched into fists. She begins shaking.

Dashon will have to dress the carcass himself and by the way his eyes crinkle she can tell that he's annoyed with her. He ropes one of the deer's back legs to a tree, exposing its belly. Then he grasps the buck's genitals and cuts the skin open, pulling the penis away from its body.

When the deer is splayed open, he hits it between its hind legs with a mallet until the bones crack. In the moonlight, the blood on his hands is not red at all, but the colour of ash. The blood steams as Dashon zippers open the deer's belly to its throat.

In Dashon's eyes she knows she must seem fickle. She had insisted on accompanying him on this hunt, and now she's recoiling at the animal's death. But when the deer inhaled his last breath, the sudden silence of the forest stole her breath away as well.

Dashon stops to sharpen his knife on the wet stone. Everything is a matter of staying sharp, dexterous, adaptable.

When the body cavity of the deer is fully open, he reaches in and grasps the stomach. It slides out easily through the opening in the belly. He lifts the deer by its hind legs to drain the body of blood. A rush of excitement causes his voice to tremor.

"My wife loves the heart," he says.

⁂

Semana Santa, as Chinchu predicted, has brought travellers to Zipolite from as far away as Veracruz, Chihuahua, Chula Vista, Orange County, and even New York. Two days into it and the restaurants have been opening early. When she walks to the beach for her swim, she tries to ignore the fools who are already drunk though it's only ten in the morning, and shouting at one another with loudspeaker voices from table to table. After she makes her deliveries in the afternoon, she returns to the beach and scrambles after shadows down to the water's edge where the sand is cooler. Today she has to hike through coconut husks, cigarette butts, the corn wrappers of half-eaten *tamales*, used condoms, abandoned towels, sun-bleached magazines, even human excrement; when she gazes out over the beach, all she can see are masses of sun-burned bodies scuttling toward the waves, dotting the shore like flies.

When she gets back to their *cabaña,* she tries to tell Chinchu the beach is so crowded she doesn't recognize it; tries to say maybe they should leave and rent a place in Puerto Angel for the week. Instead she says, "I've never really liked this place. Why do we live here again?"

"I'll take you to Veracruz if you like, it has the best seafood in Mexico."

"Today?"

"No, not today. I have rehearsal in an hour."

"How about tomorrow?"

"Be reasonable. We'll make more money this week than any other. Then we'll go to Veracruz. Or Puebla. Or Monterrey, anywhere you want."

Just this once, she wishes he would stay with her, not leave her alone while he rehearses, on this strange beach populated by unrecognizable crowds. She compels him to stay with a beloved subject, "Tell me again the story of the Aztec warriors. Please, before you go?"

He kisses her on the forehead and gathers her up in his arms. She leans her head back against his chest, nestling into him, and as he tells her about the tribal resistance to Cortes, she can smell the salt on his skin. Then he tells her about the cockfights he's seen in Chacalapa, about dances he attended as a child with his mother, in the mountains, where the wind tortured everyone's Sunday clothes and steam rose from black enamel pots against a backdrop of jagged peaks.

She pictures Dashon's wife squatting in front of the cooking fire or chasing a pig from the kitchen. She recalls how when she spoke to her husband in Mazatec, their soft-sounding words formed a veil between them and the world. Who would Dashon and his wife be in another city, in a different country, speaking a different language? She's still hunting for the right words in Spanish, searching for a way to express what she feels. But sometimes, when she can't make sense of her own feelings, she wonders if her lack of words has nothing to do with language at all.

"Chinchu, are we just going to continue . . . like this?" she asks.

"Until we're caught or the party moves elsewhere, why not?" he says, putting his guitar into his case.

Whatever she's been thinking turns into a fist in her stomach. Suddenly all she wants is a strong hand tossing her weight, digging into her thighs.

"I have to get out of here," she says.

Chinchu shrugs and picks up the guitar case. "It's all the same party."

In that moment she comprehends just how little they understand each other. What would he say if she told him she'd hoped the trip to the mountains would provide her with something solid to hold on to? That when she shot the deer, she had felt nothing inside at all? What would he say if she told him that her luck never did stand up to close examination? But somehow she doesn't have the words.

Instead she blurts out, "Are you coming home tonight?"

Chinchu frowns and pretends she hasn't spoken so that she can salvage what's left of her pride. She watches him from the bed as he gathers the rest of the things he needs – guitar picks, patch cords, and extra strings – and walks out the door without giving her the satisfaction of a backward glance. He slams the door behind him and kicks his feet in the sand, the grit of pink shells crunching under his heels.

She flicks hungrily across the still crowded beach, a bougain-villea flower tucked behind her ear, her red sarong beckon-ing like a tongue. It's still early, only seven in the evening. Around her the local children play in the sand or chase dogs spotted with cuts. The dogs chase each other down the beach, rolling coconut husks along the sand with their noses, steal-ing kicked-off sandals, running after horses.

Alone, without Chinchu by her side, she is a chameleon, moving swiftly and confidently, becoming her surroundings. Even now, she is sure she will continue to think of Chinchu as she searches the restaurants, the tables of travellers, waiting for someone to announce himself with an open mouth or the tilt of a head. At San Cristobal restaurant, a tourist trap, she presses her way to the bar, past bikini-clad women, visitors with pocket cameras, European men with their wives, whose freshly braided cornrows made them look like plucked birds.

She orders a drink and as she reaches for a handful of pesos, a man with a sunburned face offers to pay instead. She nods in thanks.

"My name's Bill. Our whole gang's here, from Wal-Mart, Guadalajara. Will you do me the pleasure?"

She lets him sit down next to her at the bar and bore her with his talk of career and family matters. She has always disliked men with red faces, loud men who make people stare and wear their testosterone like a gold chain. It is the men who challenge and taunt her, make her feel slightly uncomfortable, who excite her — the way Chinchu did in the beginning. She has always sought out the men at the vile, calm eye of a hurricane. Finally, she leaves the red-faced man behind crowing about his job and his soon-to-be ex, because his identity hinges on angle and footing, and she knows this is only half the story.

Then she hears a laugh amid the shadows of the tourists overflowing the restaurant, a laugh so sure of itself it pierces the dull sound of the waves like ice splinters.

Though the man's face is unremarkable, blending in with its setting like a snake in a mangrove swamp, it exudes a quiet magnetism. He wears a crisp linen shirt and pressed white pants. He has liquid grey eyes, sun-creased lids, and the skin of a man who has spent a lifetime in the tropics. His feet are callused, strapped into worn brown huaraches. Above interlocked hands, he rhythmically massages one thumb against the other. She brings her fingers to her throat. He has arms that can hold her tight.

"*Una Negra Modelo por favor, mi cielo.* And when you have a minute, bring me a paper also, my dear. You know how the gossip pleases me." Though the man speaks Spanish fluently, he exaggerates the American drawl, mocking his own foreignness. She sits down at his table without asking. He narrows his eyes in amusement.

The shared expectation is that whoever speaks first will lose something.

"I'm thinking of buying land here," he says finally, but in German. "By the *tortilleria*, I teach in Puebla, but I love the ocean, the hummingbirds. It will be my small statement of patriotism to the coast."

That he spoke first does not diminish the braggadocio of his words. She's familiar with this game some travellers like to play, of switching from one language to another like a merchant parading his wares. She responds in German, telling him she has also taught, some English, some French, relishing how his surprise makes his eyes twinkle. She likes who she is in German: analytical and specific.

They speak about home, the complexity of the urban Seattle metropolis he has abandoned in favour of the simplicity of Mexican sand and sky.

"Home for me isn't a place," she says. It's something she's building, she tells him, piecework, in her heart. A collection of all the things she's seen and done and smelled and tasted. "And when I've travelled widely enough, wherever I end up, then I'll have found my home." She switches to English, details her travels over the years, describing her wanderlust.

"Let's walk," he says, taking her by the hand and leading her out of the restaurant.

They stroll under a canopy of white stars that look as though they are trapped in the black sky.

"Maybe *home* is just a word for what you're looking for," he says. And she likes the feel of his fingers clamped around her wrist.

His *cabaña* lies hidden deep in the palms. He bends over and opens the padlock on his door with a key he wears around his neck.

He strokes her arms as if she is a doll while the palm fronds outside whisper against the tin roof.

"Maybe we don't know what we're looking for," she murmurs. "Or maybe some of us are never happy in one place for long. We discover that all the things we want don't come together in one place, and so we decide it's better to keep on searching."

"Maybe some of us want too much."

He lays her on the bed. From the drawer he pulls five long scarves and ties her up.

She is not allowed to touch him.

The woollen blanket scratches her writhing back. She screams, but nothing escapes the gag in her mouth. Sightlessly, she arches her body, suffocating.

The man laughs and mumbles to himself in a language she doesn't understand, its sibilance and harsh vowels catching in the back of his throat, like fish bones; she imagines him choking on them. She bites at the scarves, chafes her back raw.

After he unties her, she flees like a rabid animal, stumbling into tree trunks, wiping excrement from her eyes first with her hands, then with her shirt. Eventually, she finds herself in front of the police station, unsure of how she got to this building by the naval base. Then she's standing at the counter, with no recollection of having crossed the threshold. While she gives her statement, the station's fluorescent lights shine down on her like a cold unwanted spotlight. The officers at the counter watch her skeptically, as if she is auditioning for a role for which she is as ill-suited as she is unprepared.

A man with a chipped front tooth writes down her name. "You went with this man to his *cabaña*?"

"Yes."

"You let him tie you to the bed?"

"Yes."

He takes the form with him and walks across the room, stopping at a desk where his superior raises his eyebrows and then turns to stare at her.

She must have been out of her mind to come here. She's no longer the kind of person who can go to the police to report a crime, just as she's no longer the kind of person who might one day work in an orphanage in Chiapas. Suddenly she cares only about the stench that clings to her clothing, the sidelong glances from the people crammed on the wooden bench, waiting.

She takes a deep breath and walks out of the police station. She runs along the road to the beach, where she lets the hard waves pummel her, filling her with water as if she were a shell. She wants the ocean salt to sting her lips, her eyes to burn when she opens them. But the waves won't wash her clean; she will continue hunting for men with sweeping arms, possessing laughs, losing herself in a desire that has nothing to do with any of them.

She doesn't know for how long she swims – a minute, an hour – before she pulls herself out of the ocean and goes to a nearby taco stand, because she can't imagine going home to face Chinchu.

It's almost dawn. She sits, dripping wet, eating *pozole* while a drunken *chilango* leans unsteadily against his sweating beer, leering at her soaking wet sarong. His eyes are cold, and vacant, and sad, like the teacher's. She eats her bowl of corn soup and ignores his eyes, remembering what Juana had told her when she was last in the mountains, as they walked past the river where Juana took the goats to drink.

"You have to be careful. Just last week they found a man's body, floating here."

She asked whose body, why he was killed.

"He was from the next village. He wanted to marry a girl, but her brothers wouldn't let him, they didn't like his name."

Juana was pretending at toughness, trying to impress her with this talk.

"The world can make you strong, Juana. But be careful," she warned. "Because sometimes the world only lets you think you are tougher than you really are. Don't let the world tell you what you can do."

She tries to imagine what Chinchu will say if she tells him: *Did he hurt you? Are you sure you're okay?* Then, *You could have been killed,* and the words she least wants to hear, *Who do you think you are?* She imagines herself poised with Dashon's rifle, her finger curled around the cold trigger with the deer in her sights, and laughs. Who *did* she think she was? Chinchu would whip the man with his bicycle chain if he found out he hurt her, and, in the end, she would become nothing more than the object of his compassion and pity. Unbearable because even Juana probably knew better. Unbearable because he would be right.

She checks her body for bruises then turns to the man, still drunk, still leering. *"Look at my face,"* she says. "Tell me honestly, what do you see?"

"I see bruises, *cabrona*. Bruises. But, in the right light — who knows?"

This morning, like most mornings, she holds her hands out to Chinchu. His tongue flicking across the opium stains on her fingers is like a switch. The taste of salt burns on her tongue when she in turn licks his fingers.

She feels half-empty when she looks into his dark eyes, because the addicts are still moving into their compound, moving forward across the sand, toward the *cabaña*, and she knows they'll never stop. They'll always come back to this place, just as she and Chinchu will never leave.

Sun pierces through the bamboo slats and illuminates curls of dust spiralling from the dirt floor. They are swinging in the hammock, the rays warming their legs, twined over the criss-crossed threads like tendrils of seaweed looped together. But even as they embrace, she knows that he, too, is thinking about other bodies, the landscape of foreign places. Chinchu kisses her, his hand solid behind her neck, his mouth crushing hers, oblivious to her secret about the man with the scarves. He believed her when she told him she had a body-surfing accident. From now on, she tells him, she will always check the shoreline for hidden rocks.

Later, she counts her pesos and stacks the pawned and useless items in a corner by the bed while Chinchu restrings his guitar. Before she goes to wash her hands, she turns at the door. "I'm going to start arranging tours into the mountains, for tourists."

Chinchu stares at her for a long minute, as if trying to decide whether she is being serious or not. And then he laughs. "More deer hunters? *Híjole.*"

Once outside she stumbles toward the sickle-shaped shard of mirror nailed over the cistern, which frames her face in a canvas of bougainvillea against an amethyst sky, though it is so scratched she must squint to make out her reflection. The taste of excrement is still in her mouth though she has brushed her teeth a thousand times. She stands there and looks at her reflection as the bougainvillea petals muddy around her and people come and go. Intent as a scalpel, she watches her face take shape in the mirror, piece by piece.

She washes her hands in the water and listens to Chinchu singing. She could make it to the bus station in Pochutla before he even notices she is gone.

Last night she was at the police station.

Now she is washing almost in a trance, her mind blank except for the conviction that before moving on, one's hands should be clean.

HELEN AND FRANK

—◅═══◖ʃ◗═══▻—

H elen and Frank lived on the corner of Birch and Elm in the house with the half-moon windows. They went to church every Sunday, gave to charity, and donated blood simply because they felt it was their civic duty. Whenever the children were fighting over candy, or who got to sit shotgun in their dad's brand-new '53 Bel Air, or whose turn it was with the pedal car or the spud gun, Helen would tell them the story of how Alan had been raised from the dead.

Alan had been born just a few minutes before his twin sister, Barbara, the two of them thirteen weeks early. He had stopped breathing and turned blue in the doctor's arms. Dr. Payne (the family physician who had also delivered Alan's older sister, Eulalie, four years earlier) rolled Alan into a blanket and held the baby out to her. He asked Helen if she had picked out a name.

Helen's husband, Frank, slumped at her bedside, his head on her arm.

She took the baby from the doctor and rubbed his back. She removed his blanket and placed him on her breast, over her heart, flesh on flesh. And as she rubbed his tiny arms and legs, she told him how much she loved him. How much she wanted him. After an hour, during which no one wanted to take him away from her – she had the kind of eyes that only a mother can get, lawless, savage, spilling over with love – his limbs jerked. His eyes suddenly opened.

"Just a reaction," said the nurse flatly.

Helen, her heart flickering with hope, continued rubbing her hand back and forth across the baby's back.

Alan's eyes fluttered open again.

"Look, we get to see the colour of them before he dies," Frank said, still convinced the nurse was right.

But Alan did not die. And his eyes stayed open. Wide open. So the nurse called for the doctor. An exam was performed. Alan was sent to the prenatal ward and the whole event was pronounced a miracle.

Helen told her children this story because she hated it when they fought. "Never forget to treat each other nice," she said. "That's the meaning of the story." Because life, as she often reminded herself, especially as she was drifting off to sleep, is a fleeting miracle.

At night, Helen and Frank would lie in bed together, their feet touching under the blanket.

"I love you because you taught me to make spaghetti sauce from scratch," she would say.

"I love you because you still laugh at my jokes."

Even after they had been married sixty years, they still got dressed up and went to dances at the Legion. They danced the foxtrot. Frank could do a mean Charleston. Helen had always loved that about him. That and the way he held her hand while they danced.

At Helen's eighty-three birthday party, Alan got drunk on the wine he'd brought back from Spain the year before.

"My periodontist wants to pull them all out," Alan told his mother, talking about his teeth. "I don't know if I'm ready for dentures." Her little boy.

Eulalie had cake on her lip, where lipstick feathered into her laugh lines.

How life had flown by.

When Alan and Barbara were six, and Eulalie ten or eleven, the three children, who often played together despite their age differences, cut a sign out of cardboard. They'd used the box the clothes dryer had been delivered in to complete their project. On the homemade sign they had written in big bold black letters: "Honk! If you're happy." They took the sign to the corner of Birch and Elm, where they jumped up and down, waving the sign around.

"The new paint looks great, Dad," Alan said, pointing to the seafoam green of the living room walls.

"Thanks," said Frank, who'd done the work himself. Frank loved his home. He loved scooping maple leaves from the gutters, digging weeds out of the garden; he even enjoyed pulling hanks of hair from the bathtub drain with a clothes hanger. "A man's home is his castle" was something he often said with pride, as though more than just a common adage it was a hard-earned truth.

Just then Helen came out of the kitchen with her delicate, long-boned fingers wrapped around the stem of a crystal cake stand. She set the cake she had baked herself onto a lace doily in the centre of the dining room table.

"Ooooh," said Barbara.

"You shouldn't have gone to so much trouble, Ma," Alan said.

"Sit down, Mother," Eulalie said in tender admonishment. "You work too hard. You need to relax. I'll serve."

They ate cake and drank coffee, and the children asked Helen and Frank about the cruise their parents were taking that November.

"A European cruise, right?"

"Yes, that's right," Helen said, shooting a glance at Frank, as if confirming his approval. "With a view of the Adriatic, grey inns, window boxes full of kale, flourishing purple in the cold." Helen continued talking about the Eastern European ports of call that most excited her. Before she died, Helen wanted to see the "Pearl of the Adriatic," the twelfth-century city of Dubrovnik and its outdoor cafes. And she wanted to see Split, and the islands of Hvar, Brac, and Korcula.

Later, Eulalie took Helen into the kitchen. Frank was snoring in the corduroy easy chair, and Alan and Barbara were cheering the world heavyweight title match on TV. Eulalie wouldn't stop touching her hair with her jittery hands. Even as a baby, Eulalie had been fussy, spitting out her soothers.

And when her daughter was in high school, Helen would gaze at Eulalie's greasy hair, high cheekbones, and the pimples spotting her chin aglow in the light of the open fridge, and see in her face a sadness too old for someone so young.

"What are you looking for in there, anyway?" Helen once asked, somewhat impatiently.

Eulalie turned, slowly closed the fridge door, and lifted her eyes. "Inspiration?"

Eulalie lived in a draughty house with three dogs. Her grown son, Peter, lived off his girlfriend, who was a cashier at a discount clothing store. Eulalie often subsidised the couple's rent, just because "it was the right thing to do."

"Mom, I've got something to tell you," Eulalie said, now leaning against the stove. "I think Beth might be pregnant. The thing is, Peter hasn't come out and told me, not in so many words. But they're coming over on Sunday night."

Helen thought for a long time. On the wall above the stove hung a sampler in a frame that Helen had embroidered in high school: "A real woman brings out the best in a man." Those words had always made her shiver with pride. She was a real woman and Frank was her air and water and light. She didn't know what Eulalie wanted from her. "I was a grandma by the time I was your age."

"They don't know the first thing about being parents. I don't feel old."

"What is old supposed to feel like?" Helen asked. "I don't feel old either. Inside, I still feel like a sixteen-year-old girl."

The next day, after Helen and Frank's daughter Barbara had taken her golden retriever for a walk, she returned home and took a shower, letting the water tickle her tongue as she lifted her face to the stream. She put on her bathrobe when she was done and perched on a kitchen chair, a fresh cup of coffee in her hand, waiting for the phone to ring. Her mother had phoned her every Saturday for the past twenty years.

When the phone did not ring, Barbara put on a pair of canvas sneakers and drove to her parents' house. In the combination box by the front door, painted the same colour as the frame, was a spare key.

The half-eaten birthday cake was still sitting in the middle of the dining room table, the pile of dirty plates stacked beside it. Her mother's slippers, as if waiting for her, were still by the front door.

"There must have been something."
"Some emergency."
"Some kind of accident."
"Her slippers."
"By the front door."
"She always washes the dishes."
"The cake was still on the table."
"Not even covered."
"Not like her."
"Not at all."

Sometimes, when the children were still young, Helen and Frank would meet in the middle of the afternoon at a motel room. The place was halfway out of town, on a hill with a view of the city. The rooms had hard mattresses and carpets that smelled of cheese, and sometimes they filled the narrow pink bathtub with bubble bath. Then Helen would lead Frank, still wet from the bath, to bed.

She would unzip her duffle bag and take out a strand of pearls that dangled. With his wet body dripping, Frank would sigh as she crawled into bed, wearing just her jewellery. She grazed the nape of his neck with her chandelier earrings, skimmed her strand of pearls up and down his legs.

She loved his soft stomach, how he smelled like pine-scented candles. She loved kissing the blue veins on his feet, the crooked toe on the right foot that he'd broken in a football accident. She marvelled at its delicacy.

His hands were as big as sunfish. His hair so thick she could grab it by the fistful. And his back, with her legs twined around him, reminded her of a horse, his muscles rippling.

Afterward, lying in bed, staring at the patterns of light on the ceiling from the sun through the curtains, they'd talk.

"Barbara said she liked a *virgin* of that song 'Flip, Flop, and Fly.' Isn't that a hoot?"

"Alan fed the dog olives."

"Eulalie left late for school – again – wearing two different socks."

They'd laugh. They loved this part the best.

"Well, she wouldn't have left in her slippers."

"Yes, but – "

"But the cake."

"Yes, the cake."

"It's so odd."

"It's not like Mother."

"No. She'd never leave dirty dishes on the table."

Helen collected erasers. Ones from the five and dime; pink ones made of Indian rubber; white ones like the chewy ends of marshmallows; little ones that fit onto the end of your pencil. Then there were the ones she brought home from the elementary school where she taught. She used these on the chalkboard and brought them home still covered in a fine dust that spotted the outside of her navy blue bag.

Wearing her red slip, her feet bare, and sitting on the low upholstered chair, she would pull the erasers out from the blue bag along with the school books. "How on earth did these get in there?" she would always say when Frank caught her.

Frank said nothing. He had never understood this compulsion for collecting erasers, though he wondered if it may have been a schoolteacher thing, just a harmless quirk.

Eventually all the erasers ended up in her collection stashed under the bed.

When she retired, Helen kept the all blinds in the house closed. At first she didn't explain it to Frank, just closed the blinds whenever he opened them. Sometimes it was a game: open, closed, open, closed. A way of communicating without words, like signalling in semaphore. But Frank didn't know what Helen was signalling. Only that when she was grumpy, the house was darker. On her better days, she might open one window a crack. She was all action, no message.

"I'm embarrassed," she said finally. "By how I look now. I hate mirrors."

"So that's why you're closing the blinds?"

He held her close to him with his large hands. Her hair felt like feathers. "Kiddo, you make me laugh." But as he held her, he could feel her whole body shaking. She was crying, without making a sound.

On the night of their senior prom, Frank had driven Helen to Lookout Point in his dad's Packard. He guided her through a forest of bracken fern down a narrow path. The promontory was still and quiet and they sat on a bald rock that looked like a hand as it jutted out over the farms below. Despite the moonlight, the land before them was dark and Helen arranged her prom dress to cover her ankles against the cold night air.

"I've got two cupcakes that I stole from the dance," Frank said, reaching into the pocket of his suit jacket. Tiny rose-buds folded into a paper napkin. The icing had fallen off in his pocket.

He was the cutest boy in school. Maybe she would kiss him.

When she took a bite of the cupcake, he watched her chin quiver. He knew he wanted to spend his life with her.

They talked about school and friends and plans for their summer and for their lives ahead. Her blond hair shone in the moonlight. The air was perfumed by her shampoo.

"Tell me something you've never told anyone before," he said. "Tell me a secret."

Frank's hand on her shoulder was warm and comforting, the way bathwater is after a long, cold day outside. And because he made her feel surrounded by warmth she said, "I was born with three ears."

His eyes flicked to her hair and then he looked down quickly, embarrassed by what he'd done.

Helen placed his hand on her hair. "Silly. I don't still have three ears. The doctors took it off when I was born. But, if you touch me, here – feel this part right *here* – maybe you can feel the scar."

He felt dizzy at her touch, and the sight of the creamy whiteness of her neck when she tilted her head toward him almost made him faint. He nuzzled his nose over where he imagined the scar to be. "If I asked you to kiss me, would you?"

Helen giggled.

Emboldened, Frank said, "I love you."

She smiled. "That's silly. Try to kiss me."

"Oh. I just wanted to know if you'd say yes." He paused. "By the way, are you going to eat that second cupcake?"

"You! You!" she yelled. Then they were chasing each other around Lookout Point in the dark, miles above the farms that seemed to stretch on forever in the moonlight.

When Frank was twenty-one, his entire engineering class was commandeered by the Canadian Officer Training Corp and for six months they marched up the university's football field in their civvies, there not being enough uniforms to go around. Most of his friends were excited that they were training to kill Nazis instead of studying for mid-terms. Frank was not. A week before leaving for Normandy, Helen sat with him in her mother's backyard. She was pulling blades of grass out of the ground and dropping them onto her saddle shoes. "I want to have a baby," she said suddenly.

His stomach flipped in a pleasant way. Frank reminded her that he was leaving soon.

She wiped her hands, and they stayed green. "I don't want to wait. Look how goddamn beautiful everything is. Every day that goes by is another goddamn day he's missing."

The bridge of her nose, the way her long eyelashes brushed against the lenses of her glasses, her delicate collarbone, the nape of her neck covered in fine blond down, everything seemed to point at his staying.

But of course he couldn't. It was war.

He went to France, returned, married Helen, continued his studies, and became an engineer.

When Helen was pregnant with the twins, she often took Eulalie to the park. And while Eulalie played, Helen would shift her weight, putting her magazine on the grass, and she'd lean onto her on her side in the dappled sunlight next to the red playground slide. "When you two move inside me late at night," she would tell the twins, "and there's nothing but the sound of your daddy's breathing, it feels like the three of us are floating up in space."

Five days went by. Alan and Barbara and Eulalie smoked, stared out windows, and made endless pots of coffee in each other's kitchens as they waited for the phone to ring.

"It means they were coming right back. The cake and the slippers."

"Coming right back, just stepping out for a single moment."

"Yes."

"The slippers waiting for her, set just so, beside the door."

"As if she was only going to be gone a second."

"Yes, that's it. Just a second."

"Look," Alan interjected, "someone's got to say it. People who want to kill themselves don't repaint their house or buy tickets for a holiday cruise."

Helen and Frank had booked their passage for a fourteen-day Adriatic cruise leaving from Venice in November. They kept the tickets on the dresser next to the framed picture of them on their wedding day. Helen gazed at the tickets whenever she brushed her hair.

She imagined how, after the stopover in Dubrovnik, all the Italian papers would report on the Canadian couple who had locked their cabin, hung a do-not-disturb sign on their door, stepped out onto their balcony and, holding hands, let themselves fall into the sea. The part of the pact Helen disliked the most was dying so far from her children. But Frank had decided their dying at home would cause the children too much trouble, emotional and legal, especially if any of them were to assist Helen and Frank at their bedsides in the double suicide they had been planning.

At her birthday party, Helen never mentioned they had cancelled their Adriatic cruise.

A few weeks before, their doctor of thirty years had given them the bad news that Frank was dying. And even though he talked about cutting-edge treatments for colon cancer, Helen and Frank both knew there was a possibility that Frank might not make it to November.

"How long do I have, Bill?"

The doctor turned to Frank. "There's no such thing as mathematics when it comes to life and death. Not even I have a guarantee I'll make it home tonight."

"You know that's not what I mean."

"Frank, I can't say a month or a year. There are so many exceptions in both directions. So just don't ask me that." His eyes were full of tears as he looked away.

When Frank had gone to work as a torpedo man during the Second World War, Helen had been forced to stare down the black-eyed, hollow barrel of the universe for the first time. Now, she could once again feel the weight of her sadness keeping her in bed, pushing her eyelids shut so she couldn't get up, get dressed, do anything, not even think.

One night shortly before her eighty-third birthday, she said to Frank, "Does the universe think I don't love you enough? Is that it?" She realized, even as she said it, how ridiculous it was to equate true love with forever. Love wasn't everything: nothing was everything. *Nothing* was everything.

"Let's go for a drive."

Helen had been gathering plates and forks from the dining room table, scraping the leftover crumbs and icing from each plate onto the one she had set aside, on which she also piled the dirty forks.

"Leave those."

"It'll just take a minute."

"Leave them. For once."

The word *once* came down hard as a hammer stroke. Yes, thought Helen, for once in her life she would set the plate in her hand back onto the table. She'd leave the half-eaten birthday cake right in the middle of the table, surrounded by crumbs and the remaining mess from the party.

She'd put on her shoes and take a drive.

As they passed the turn-off for the casino, they neared the site of their first date.

"Let's go," he said. "For old times' sake."

The dusty gravel road that sliced through the wide belt of land between the Ghost and Red Deer Rivers was used only by mining and logging trucks. The sign read, "Road not recommended for travel," but they have travelled it too many times to be bothered by its message, ignoring it on their first date and on the night of their senior prom and on all their subsequent visits to Lookout Point.

Frank slows the car. They both look at each other. In a hundred years the road will be grown over with ferns. Everyone they know will be gone.

He pulls over the car under the shorn light of the moon. Then, changing his mind, he puts the car back in gear and advances it a little farther down the banked edge into the scrub brush where it will be hidden by foliage.

"Let's go."

"To the lookout?"

He stares straight into the thicket of evergreen.

"Really?"

He shrugs. Unbuckles his seat belt.

Helen blinks at him, because he's parked in the brambles where it will be difficult for her to get out of the car. But when he trains his cannon-shot eyes at her, she feels her cheeks grow red. He can still make her blush, sixty years on. They've been to this lookout many times, as teenagers, and then frequently before the kids were born. A few times after that, even, when their family was still young. But they haven't been back in many years.

He steps out of the car, pushing the branches aside for her so that she can get out too.

Her fingers tingle.

From his pocket Frank pulls a flashlight. He has always liked surprises.

One day, for no reason at all, Frank sent her two dozen pink roses in the middle of winter. Sometimes he pulls the car over just to give her a kiss.

She isn't afraid, in spite of the sweat on her brow, the hair in her mouth, and her glasses slipping. It's just that she's having a hard time keeping up with him. The snow is hard to walk in.

"Wait," she says, "my glasses. They're lost."

Frank sighs. "You need them?"

"I'd like to see."

"All right."

Frank gets down on his hands and knees and so does Helen. The flashlight quavers over snow that is wetter and heavier than usual, and Helen can feel the damp of it soaking into her stockings, coating her knees. She pats the snow trying to find them, hoping she doesn't crush them.

"Found them," Frank says.

"Thank you," she says.

She follows, pushing on against the snow, over the slippery carpet of pine needles and fallen leaves underneath.

At times Frank will stretch out his hand behind him, as he has always done, waiting for her to take it.

Helen notices they have arrived in a grove of sorts, cedars armouring the path. The evergreens look as if they've been uprooted and dipped in snow.

She slumps against the base of a cedar tree whose trunk is about as wide as a cradle.

Helen delivered the twins at twenty-seven weeks, when the babies were just the size of sparrow's nests.

"Gone?" Helen said to the doctor, who stood there shaking his head. "It can't be."

"Have you chosen a name?" the doctor asked.

"Alan," she said. "We had decided on Alan."

He passed Alan to her and when she unwrapped his blanket, his arms and legs flopped like a jellyfish — *lifelessly,* she thought — onto her chest, where she placed him over her heart.

Frank sobbed at the edge of her bed. "It's okay," she said to him, "it's okay." And to Alan, she whispered in his ear how much she loved him, how much she wanted him. "You were so wanted."

"Helen," Frank said, pointing at his eyes, "they're staying open."

The nurse called it a reflex; but later, the doctors called it a miracle.

She closes her eyes. It's warmer now.

Frank watches Helen as she sleeps. His little girl. He parts her hair and kisses the scar that marks where a third ear had been long ago. For a moment he wonders if he should carry her back to the car. But the car doesn't have enough gas to make it back to the main road and would be as cold as an icebox anyway. Besides from this vantage point as long as he's awake he can see the moon.

"But what were they doing in the woods?"

"Maybe they got lost," Alan said. "Maybe they turned left instead of right. They were out of gas."

"But what on earth were they doing in the forest?"

"If they were lost why didn't they stay with the car?"

Barbara said, "I like to think they weren't scared."

Tiphaine had bought El Principe at Chato's insistence. After a two-week vacation, he'd serpent-tongued her into spending her life savings to buy the resort. He'd whispered into her neck — making her hair stand on end — that he would never leave her side so long as she laid her heart at his feet. He said things like that, making her feel as though her life was romantically scripted. In Paris, working as a secretary, Tiphaine had been hopeful, if not happy. But she had not been extraordinary. Though she had only known Chato a few weeks, she had returned to Paris, sold her apartment, and doubled back to Honduras to marry him.

Mostly, she didn't regret her choices.

The resort, which was nothing more than a thatch hut that tilted in the sand, was cool and shady, with bikinis and beach towels drying on the bamboo fence that encircled it.

A waist-high counter set the kitchen apart from the restaurant, which was filled with wooden tables stained with candle wax and covered with oyster-shell ashtrays. Hammocks for rent overnight swung along both sides of the building. Through the lifeless remains of almond trees, you could see a corner of the ocean that resembled a white sheet tied on all four sides to docks and cays. In the distance, pelicans dove for fish in a bay as smooth as a pane of glass while local children pushed each other off a trestle bridge.

The tourists who stayed in Cayo Bonaire came to sneak from life more than it had to give. It was a town of hot sky and listless dories, green crabs scurrying across the road, pizzerias painted yellow and red guarded by men holding semi-automatic rifles. It was a town where the fronds of palm trees waving in lazy breezes were sometimes the fastest moving things around. Still, it tempted all comers, like a woman who lets her hair down at dusk.

The beach shared with the town both its grit and its wild beauty, and on Tiphaine's days off, she would sit on one of the logs scattered along the beach and gaze down the far-reaching length of it. Today, the wind was blowing sand onto her legs, pelting her skin, reminding Tiphaine of the sting of fire ants. Beside her Chato rolled a joint, turning his back to the wind to protect the marijuana as he broke up the buds into the brown curl of a dried banana leaf.

Earlier that day, while balancing the accounts after breakfast, Tiphaine and Chato had had another one of their fights.

"You can't put three extra nights on his tab," Chato said.

"Why not?" Tiphaine answered. "Three nights. Five. What difference does it make? The tourists are all too busy being on vacation to notice. Besides, you make enough money selling them drugs. What do you care if I have a piece?"

Tiphaine tried to block the memory of the argument the same way she tried to ignore the silver bodies of dead fish glinting on the sand. But even after she drained her can of beer to the last drop, she couldn't hide from their eyes like open wounds, pale in their sockets. She trained her focus instead on Sebastian toddling to and fro across the beach, scooping handfuls of wet sand from the water's edge and launching them like grenades.

Last week, after being woken by the whoops of tourists, Tiphaine had sat up and been unable to spot Sebastian on the beach. Here the tide was known to pull things out to sea. Eventually, she'd found him beyond the boulders, splashing knee-deep in water. It was a miracle, really, that he hadn't drowned. But Tiphaine had to fight the squeezing sensation in her chest at the memory because she didn't want anything to ruin this day. They had left the cooks in charge of the resort, and Sebastian was now lying on his back, looking up at the blue sky, making starfish shapes in the sand.

Two of Chato's friends came by and sat on the log next to him, and they shared a bottle of cane liquor. Tiphaine chucked her empty beer can toward the growing pile by the river that divided the beach in two. Sebastian tottered toward the pile and thrust his thumb into the mouth of one of the cans and held it up in the air, thumbs up. Her happy boy. He could play with a piece of garbage like that for hours.

In Paris, parents were always fussing over their children, putting them in sun-proof aqua suits and rubber-soled beach shoes, covering what skin was left exposed with chemically laden sunscreen, the thicker the better, as if they were icing a cake. People here did not fuss over their children in the same way, thought Tiphaine. Here, Sebastian was learning to speak the language of the sand, learning the sensation of the sun on his collarbone, the wind at his elbows. He would grow into the easy ways of men who always went shirtless and never wore shoes. He would never have an ordinary life.

"*Chingame,*" Chato swore. He twisted the edges of the banana leaf together then tried to seal them with spit. Still, the joint came apart. He held the package of mottled leaf toward Tiphaine accusingly.

"You didn't bite the leaf enough," she said. "You must really bite down on the edges before you roll it." She mimicked a beaver with her teeth. "Its brokenness keeps it whole. I don't know why you insist on using banana leaf instead of rolling papers anyway. It's —"

"Natural and free."

"So pretentious."

Tiphaine finished rolling the joint for him. When she was done, she stared out across the beach at the tourists, most of them students on break from universities around the globe, ersatz adventurers, soul-seekers, and hayseed gurus. They frolicked topless in the ocean and swayed in encampments bounded by driftwood, the music from their guitars and didgeridoos mingling with the lapping waves. Farther down the beach, a row of overturned fishing dories provided shade for some local teenagers, knobby knees peeking out from under the whitewashed wood, an edge of navy-and-white uniform, the legs of adolescent girls always brave and horse-like.

Farther down still, four Catholic Miskito women bathed fully clothed, their waist-length braids flashing in the white heat.

Sebastian was waving the empty beer can over his head while Chato's friends laughed, their mouths full of brown teeth. They were the sons of fishermen whose fathers were fishermen, and when they looked at her – a blond French woman, an ex-pat – she wondered what they saw. She preferred to think she was different from the other foreigners, who were too arrogant or sheepishly fawning, proud or embarrassed by their privileged lot. While the locals went to cockfights and the newcomers did yoga, she did neither, preferring to keep her mind on her business and tend to Sebastian when she could.

Sebastian waddled toward a pile of driftwood. Friday was market day for his nanny, Olivia. Sebastian spent most of his time with Olivia, either down at the beach or playing in the resort's courtyard, where a pet deer was tied to the mango tree. And though Tiphaine told herself to be happy that her son loved his nanny, she sometimes worried that he might be growing too attached to her. The thought gnawed at Tiphaine, but what choice did she have? A woman running her own business needed a nanny. She tried to push the doubts from her mind. There would be enough criticism of her parenting skills once her mother-in-law arrived from Tegucigalpa tomorrow. Then she'd see even less of her son. Luz took over the whole house and demanded all of Chato's and Sebastian's attention whenever she visited. Though it hurt Tiphaine to be relegated to being an outsider in her own home, what could you say to a man whose mother could do no wrong in his eyes?

Sebastian's diaper was sagging down to his knees as he ran along the shoreline. Even from where she sat she could see that his chubby legs, with their folds so deep she could lose her fingers inside them, were crusted in filth. She was thinking she should get up and change his diaper when he started to wail, the sound slowly growing in pitch. It was a cry Tiphaine hadn't heard since his colicky-baby phase, when he had screamed through the night in a hammock woven out of plastic shopping bags that hung from the rafters of their house, suspended by two ropes. Not knowing what to do and anxious for Chato to return from wherever he claimed to be, Tiphaine had huddled in the farthest corner of the room and chewed her fingers, listening to Sebastian's demanding cries, her muscles growing more rigid by the hour, until Chato finally opened the door. She hated his finding her in the corner like that, and seeing his anger, his disappointment in her, she had sworn she'd do better. More times than she'd like to admit she'd made this promise to herself only to break it again and again.

As usual, Chato reached Sebastian first, scooping the boy into his arms and kissing his face. As he cuddled his son, Chato spoke into the boy's ear, in quiet confidence, two men sharing a joke. "Oh *pobrecito*, you poor little thing. I'm here. Your mother's too drunk to look after you right."

Had it not been for Chato's friends, watching her with curious faces, she might have crumpled and sank to her knees. It wasn't right. It wasn't right at all for Chato to be saying these things. Who was he to be judging her?

Chato held the toddler out to her. In the end, it was a mother's work to look after a child. Impatience simmered behind Chato's smile as she took Sebastian from his arms and examined the boy's cut. It was nothing, a small wound where the mouth of the tin had cut into his thumb. She nestled her son against her hip. "Hush, hush, hush. You're a brave boy. Why are you crying?"

"*Chinga a tu pinche madre.*" Chato laughed in derision for the benefit of his friends. "She doesn't care if he bleeds and dies."

As though sensing a shift in the mood of the day, Chato's friends tried to calm her: "It's nothing, *mamacita.*" And, "It's not good for a mother to be too overprotective."

Tiphaine nodded and smiled. "See there. Shhh, shhh." After a minute, the blood had stopped trickling down Sebastian's arm. She touched her tongue to the red line, first licking then wiping it away with the hem of her skirt.

Chato cracked open another beer and raised it toward his friends. "My father beat me so many times I can't remember. The hospital in Tegus has a list this long with my injuries. The one I still remember is 'beaten over the head with a tequila bottle.' But every time I got up." He was staring Tiphaine down, as if to challenge her.

Tiphaine felt weak. She had never told anyone that some days just looking at Chato turned her inside out, her love barrelling through her with a hurricane force that left her feeling uprooted. The sheer strength of her love for him startled her, even as she suspected there were limits to his.

She hushed, hushed Sebastian, softening his cries to whimpers. Then she put his thumb in her mouth and sucked on the soft flesh until he began to sleep, his weight hot in her lap, his head heavy against her breast.

∂𝒫

If Chato could earn money from the tourists, why couldn't she?

Tiphaine watched the girl with dreadlocks, lying alone in her hammock, pretending to rest although her eyes were wide open. The girl was watching the other guests eating or playing chess, her gaze stubborn yet hungry, on the lookout for something beyond the green palms full of coconuts or the fish splayed open, flat as postcards, drying in the street just beyond the bamboo fence. A few years ago, Tiphaine had worn the same intense expression under a floppy straw hat, sketching in a book full of pencil-coloured seashells. Tipahine sat sideways in the next hammock, her rum eye-opener between her knees, and held out a pack of Belmont Filtros.

"You like the beach?" Tiphaine asked as the girl took a cigarette.

She nodded. "The food's great, too."

"And the beer's cheap."

Tiphaine told the girl she owned the place and, as usual, was met with disbelief. Why, Tiphaine was too young! It couldn't be true.

Kirstie and her sister, both Spanish majors, were from Antwerp. Tiphaine had checked the girls in yesterday and booked their hammocks for three weeks. Kirstie wore her blond hair in dreadlocks through which she had woven strands of coloured wool. Streaks of zinc whitened the freckled skin on the bridge of her nose and cheeks, giving her sunburned face the look of half-ripe fruit. Next to Kirstie's raw innocence, her sister, Marie, with her dark hair and skin the colour of acacia bark, struck Tiphaine as exotic and almost world-weary in comparison. Tall and ropy, Marie gazed out at the world through heavily-lidded eyes.

"Yes, we have different fathers," Kirstie said, rocking back and forth in her hammock.

As she spoke, Kirstie's eyes settled on the young man squeezing orange juice by the sinks; on his lean, perfect body, his hips revealed by shorts worn provocatively low. There was an expression of desire on the girl's face that made Tiphaine wince; it was typical of Cayo Bonaire tourists to wear their appetites so openly, as they tried to pack it all in – excitement, sex, drugs, suntans – as if stuffing items in a suitcase. To think she'd ever been one of them.

"He lives to love women," Tiphaine finally said, lowering her head conspiratorially. "It's what he does, if you *know* what I mean."

Would she like to? Tiphaine asked.

Kirstie threw her head back as she laughed, her dread-locks bouncing in the air with the motion. Then she turned to look at him again.

Five months ago, Austin had run out of money while backpacking. Instead of going home to Clifton, Arizona, he'd rented a shack farther down the beach with no electricity, using his wristwatch for collateral, and lived off oranges. Then he started running drugs for Chato. The day Tiphaine had hired him to work at El Principe – this boy with his slim waist and avocado-green eyes – she'd walked to his shack with some cocaine hidden in her floppy straw hat, expecting just another one of Chato's lackeys. But what she found surprised her: a copy of William Blake, a set of wood-carving tools, and a sack of oranges on a table he'd built himself from pieces of driftwood he'd found on the beach. She took out an orange and ate it while sitting next to him, cross-legged on the ground.

Tiphaine had offered him room and board in exchange for doing odd jobs, and now Austin lived in the space they'd built behind the resort for extra storage but never used. He squeezed the orange juice and cleaned the toilets.

When Kirstie said yes, Tiphaine told her to approach Austin as she would any man to whom she was sexually attracted. Touch his arm. Don't be shy. Raise your eyes then lower them again. Coy, but not too coy. Say "I like you," simply, with her fingers brushing his.

"But you must listen to me very carefully. There's a certain way to approach this situation. A certain kind of. . . . decorum. Never mention money. Never mention you are paying for his services." And Kirstie nodded as if she'd known this all along.

Tiphaine put Kirstie's money in her pocket and watched as the girl sauntered toward Austin. A bus belching black exhaust fumes stopped in front of El Principe, its roof piled high with bundles of produce, bolts of cloth, and huge mesh bags. A tourist peered out through the dusty glass panes, and orange-laden boys in torn shirts and bare feet were already gathering around to offer up their riches to the windows.

As Tiphaine made her way to the bar to serve the travellers, she glanced back at Austin and the girl. She wasn't sure if she was taking advantage of a fool, or if it was no different than charging admission to the ocean. Austin was a young man with a libido. As far as she was concerned, it was as natural for him to make love as it was for a canary to sing, whether or not it was being watched.

Still, it was only a matter of time before he found out, before she was caught. Passing beers across the counter, she wondered how long she would have to wait.

That evening, a group of German tourists showed up at the house asking for Chato. Tiphaine invited the men in and let them play with Sebastian as she called El Principe, but Chato was nowhere to be found. When she grew tired of waiting for Chato and impatient to lose herself, she retrieved Chato's personal stash. The Germans had come to Central America for the cheap cocaine, and she sold them what Chato had taped to the underside of the toilet tank lid, trying to hide it from her. In gratitude, they let her snort coke with them until dawn.

After they left, she sat chewing her nails, watching Sebastian doze fitfully after crying himself to sleep, and waited for the alarm clock to go off. Grey clouds slowly crept across the sky, and it began to rain. Then a crack-roar of thunder sent cats scurrying under houses and dogs scratching at doors to get in. Sitting by the window, Tiphaine heard the green palms whisper, snap, and shake, as the now-purple sky flashed with lightning. When she had first come to Cayo Bonaire, she had been overwhelmed by the rain – the sheer force of it as it washed over her, threatening to sweep her away as if she were nothing more than a pebble in a river, while flooding houses, causing mudslides, unmooring trees. Yet its daily siege had overcome her until, worn down, she no longer had the necessary resistance to truly fear its power. The tropical rains became just a rhythm outside her window; let it hammer on the roof tiles or shake the walls, her fight was gone.

By the time the alarm went off at 7:30, the storm had stopped as suddenly as it had started. Tiphaine rose to turn off the alarm, feeling a gnawing ache in every part of her body. As she tried to shake off her drug-induced reverie, she dressed Sebastian then muscled him, kicking and squirming, into his stroller.

When she arrived at El Principe, Tiphaine found the cooks cleaning up in the aftermath of the storm. Guests were wringing water from their beach towels and some of the local boys thrust fallen palm leaves at each other like swords. Chato was drinking beer and playing poker with Austin at one of the restaurant tables.

"Where were you?" she shouted, as she pushed Sebastian's stroller toward Chato as if in accusation. "All these customers showed up at the house last night and you weren't there to take care of them. I called everywhere trying to find you. Where were you?"

"I have enough to worry about with people wanting their money back because their hammocks got wet."

"Yes, I can see you are busy."

The cooks in the kitchen glanced at one another knowingly over their chopping boards. Resort guests raised their heads from their hammocks or turned from their breakfasts to watch the commotion. Austin fanned his cards and tried to pretend Tiphaine was not standing in front of him, her nose running, her hair in tangles. The wet roads had muddied her flip-flops and her painted toenails. He had never seen her looking so pitiful.

Chato was telling Tiphaine to mind her own business; he'd had things to take care of last night. From the way her body quivered, Austin knew the thin edge of rage on which she balanced was tipping.

"If it wasn't for me," she was saying, "just look around. If it wasn't for me —"

Chato glanced up again from the cards in his hand. "What? You think because you sold the little bit you stole from me you're a businesswoman? You partied with them like a girl for hire. Don't look so shocked. When I saw the Germans this morning they complimented me on what a fun wife I have. But you could never manage the deals I do. Our profits would be up your nose if I let you. If I can't even trust you not to dip into a tiny stash, how can I trust you with anything else?"

Chato slammed his beer down so hard the liquid foamed in the bottle and bubbled over the lip. The brief silence that followed was broken by Sebastian's wails. Tiphaine picked him up and tried to quiet him, but he pushed her away, mashing his hands into her face.

"You want to be responsible for everything," she said, "but you are not responsible at all. Not even for your own son."

"Is that so? Then why he is squirming in your arms like he wants to get away?"

She crumpled then, and looked so small that Austin suddenly wished he could reach out to defend her. A ray of sun illuminated her blond hair and the halo of light that surrounded her made her appear even more uncertain. She closed her eyes and breathed in and out slowly. After a moment she said, "There was coke there in front of me, in little piles everywhere. I waited but you never came. What were you doing that was so urgent?"

Chato's eyes glinted then, but as if thinking better of it, he shook his head and pointed with his beer toward the kitchen instead. "Why don't you make yourself busy with something important."

"While you just sit there and drink more beer. Good. Be drunk when your mother arrives. She'll be happy to see that."

Chato just laughed and picked up his cards. "Play," he ordered Austin.

She wouldn't get near his stash again, Chato was saying after Tiphaine left in a fury with Sebastian. From now on he would keep his personal supply on him, but with the money Austin was earning her, who knew what trouble she might get herself into.

"What are you talking about?" Austin said.

"Come, *m'ijo*. My son. Don't play the fool. It's so obvious you like my wife. She's pretty, *a poco no?*"

"Everyone likes your wife." Not until Chato snorted in amusement did Austin realize his words had come out wrong.

"If you are trying to tell me you don't know what is going on, then you are even more of a fool than I thought." Chato took a long guzzle from his beer.

"Why don't you tell me, then, Chato. Come on, tell me why I'm a fool."

Chato told Austin that Tiphaine had been pimping him for almost two months.

"Nothing goes on without me knowing about it," Chato said defiantly. "And I know everything about my wife." He was a man laying his cards on the table, victorious.

Then, as if in consolation, his voice as smooth as a scalpel, Chato said, "It's just a little fun." He got up and slapped

Austin on the back as he left the table. "Some hot, spicy, Caribbean fun. And no one gets hurt, right?"

The boy felt bruised, his ego wounded: twelve women in less than two months; it only seemed strange in hindsight. Even the bet he'd made with Chato last week, to see who could sleep with more women before the season was out, now seemed a cruel joke. Austin had wanted to be like Chato, who had only to spread his fingers, it seemed, for his hands to be filled. Maybe if he was patient, he thought, he too could live in a whitewashed house within a grove of lime trees, with a wife like Tiphaine. Austin carried his love for Tiphaine everywhere. Whenever he was with a woman, she was always there, just beyond those nameless curves. Tiphaine, Tiphaine, Tiphaine, whose name he sometimes grunted, without any control.

Now he was their dupe. The shame he felt was lodged inside him, as if he'd swallowed a bone or eaten something spoiled.

He spent the rest of the day rocking himself in a hammock, smoking endless joints, trying to decide what to do. The nylon had etched its way deep into his flesh by the time he got up because he could no longer stand the flies. Dusk was coming on; he could hear the sounds of showers running and toilets being flushed with buckets of water from the cistern. The smell of bug spray clung to the humid air, wafting off the legs of young women going to one of the beach-front bars to dance and drink. He heard a familiar voice and glanced up from his hammock to see Kirstie push open the gate, hips swaying seductively as she crossed the sand and settled herself into one of the rental hammocks by the bar.

"Hey. Let me ask you something," Austin said, hopping into the empty hammock beside her. He hoped to find the words that would make the hard question he wanted to ask come across easy and joking.

"Did I *pay* Tiphaine for you?" Kirstie giggled and started to search through her backpack, taking out a bottle of sunscreen, a pocket camera, a cigarette lighter, and a Dutch fashion magazine as if to divert his attention. She laid these on the sand and looked at them as though they belonged to someone else.

"Come on," he said, pushing through his shame. "How much? It's a game Tiphaine and I play."

Kirstie stared at Austin intently, as if calculating what he might do. "Then, you should guess."

"I don't want to guess. Just tell me."

Eventually she whispered, "Twenty American dollars."

As Austin let the information sink in, he asked if she was enjoying Honduras and listened distractedly as she told him of her travels so far.

"Me and Marie? Yesterday we hitchhiked to Santa Rosa . . . I got a tattoo, see?" She lifted up her shirt and showed him a small sun tattooed around her belly button. "I traded the guy a gram of coke for it, so it was only half the price it would've been if I'd paid in cash."

"Where did you get the coke?"

"Marie met up with Chato last night in Santa Rosa, so I got him to give me some at a good price. It's the first time I've been high."

"And did you enjoy it?" It was hard to keep the disgust from his voice.

"They're meeting again in a few days, at an Italian restaurant called Geminis. Do you want to come with me? I could buy some more."

Earlier that day, Tiphaine had been whitewashing the trunks of palm trees with Olivia when she glanced back at the restaurant and saw Luz coming toward them with Sebastian on her hip. He was playing with his grandmother's earrings, flicking them with his pudgy fingers. Luz, with her expertly pencilled lips and pantsuits and stylish short hair. Behind them, Tiphaine could just make out Chato sitting at the bar, but she'd already spent her anger. She felt the same sadness that sluiced through her veins since Sebastian's birth; it surged and found release only when she got high then poured out into the open whenever she was coming down. She was exhausted from staying up all night with the Germans, and she couldn't stop the paint brush from shaking in her hand.

Sebastian slid down from Luz's hip and ran with his arms out, airplaning up to Olivia, who lifted him up in her arms. The little boy smiled at Tiphaine, showing her his small pearl teeth. Oh, how she adored her son. This close to him it seemed easier to breathe. She tickled him until he gasped. "*Ma puce.* You're such a silly *puce.* I love you."

"*Dale un beso a tu mama,*" Olivia said, tucking his hair behind his ear.

But Sebastian did not want to kiss Tiphaine.

"No." He shook his head violently.

Olivia tilted him toward his mother once again.

"No!" Sebastian giggled and shrieked.

Luz hesitated for a moment, but then couldn't stop the words from charging out. "A mother," she said, "should spend more time with her children."

Tiphaine wiped her forehead, leaving a wet streak she could feel on her skin. "I didn't ask for your opinion, Luz."

"Hah! Just keep thinking you know what's best. Keep thinking you know and we'll see!"

Tiphaine set her paintbrush on top of the bucket and couldn't think of anything to do but reach out and tickle him again.

"It's good thing I'm so busy today. Now you won't miss a minute with him."

"Yes, we have fun, don't we?" Luz said to Sebastian, taking him away from Olivia and nuzzling his neck. She laughed. "Tiphaine, you should remember you don't become a mother just by having a child."

Luz's words continued to buzz in Tiphaine's head hours later, as she trailed listlessly behind Austin through the night market, where vendors hawked shampoo or merengue cassettes, and little boys with black polish and rags and lungs like Pavarotti sang out for shoes to shine. Tiphaine cowered whenever Luz came to visit, often retreating from her own home by finding chores at El Principe that needed to be done to excuse her absence. She felt useless in the face of the cruel competence with which Luz could run any household, especially one as barely managed as Tiphaine's. No one needed her: not her burned cooking nor her nursery songs. Then again, what mother wouldn't give her son everything he asked for? A terrible mother, like her.

She had left halfway through preparing dinner.

"I'll finish it for you," Luz said, smiling as she stirred the brown Mexican mole sauce that Tiphaine had always hated but Chato loved. Yet it was a smile that said, "Because only then will I know it's done right."

Chato admonished her. His mother was in town. What could she be thinking by leaving?

"I have to go to the market tonight. I forgot something. Ingredients for a special order that the cooks need tomorrow for breakfast."

"This is an emergency?"

"I have to go," she said. Then she had gotten into her car and driven away.

Now, Tiphaine watched as Austin walked just ahead of her through the crowd, drifting past stalls heaped with mountains of plantain and pineapple, behind which women with their black hair parted down the middle gossiped about the men in their family. She was glad Austin was here with her tonight. Their frequent jaunts to the night market had become one of the high points of her week. Admiring the ease with which he fended off beggars or bargained with vendors, she was reminded again of how different he was from the other tourists; he was looking for something deeper than a holiday fling or a pocketful of postcards or a drug-fuelled adventure to keep from his parents and to brag about to friends. Austin had chosen to stay here in Honduras, just as she had. The difference was, unlike her, he could still leave.

"Austin, how much longer do you think you'll stay here?" Tiphaine asked, cutting open a bag of limes with a knife. She was standing in the kitchen at El Principe in her bare feet while Austin carried the market groceries to the table.

"College will still be there when I go back," he said, unloading watermelons, oranges, tortillas, and chickens with hard-to-pluck pinfeathers still dirtying their wings. "If I decide to go back."

Something in his voice was sharp. There was a new force in the way he spoke to her, so changed from his usual fumbling awkwardness. Distracted, she let the bag slip from her hands, the limes spilling across the floor. Austin got on the ground with her to pick them up and when her tank top slipped forward, revealing the top of her breasts, she smiled at him.

He smiled back, baring his teeth, his expression more wolfish than she was used to from him. Caught off-guard, Tiphaine started putting the limes back into the bag.

"God, it's late," she said, to break the tension. "I don't want to go back home, but Chato's mother is probably saying terrible things about me. What do you call a mother who eats her young?"

"So stay."

"I will, I think," she said, feeling strangely rudderless. "At least until she falls asleep." Sebastian would already be in bed by now, curled up under his mosquito net. Had he even noticed she was gone?

"You should be glad you don't have a mother-in-law," she continued, retrieving two bottles of beer from the industrial-sized cooler and a glass from the cupboard for herself. She set down a beer in front of Austin. She leaned back in her seat and stretched her legs out in front of her so they reached under the table, near his feet. "But maybe you want a wife, no? The two go together. Yet I can't imagine you married."

He jerked his beer off the table, anger sparkling in his eyes, but he didn't say a word.

"Don't you have a date tonight?" she said, wanting to push him. She poured her beer into her glass. She found his silence unsettling. Did he suspect something?

"Naw. No one wants me tonight." He gazed at her steadily as he spoke.

For long minutes, Austin and Tiphaine sat quietly together at the table; him, scheming, her, exiled from her own house.

Watching his sun-cracked lips close around the mouth of the bottle, she was uncertain if she had done wrong by him. *Guilt.* She lit a cigarette and blew a smoke ring into the air, tried to banish the feeling by submerging herself in the sound of the conga drums playing somewhere in the distance. But her guilt continued to swirl within her just as the beer swirled in her glass, her hand shaking. She had never felt this hollow.

"There is a new Italian restaurant in Santa Rosa," Austin said at last.

Above them, the bare light bulb torched the wings of clumsy moths.

"Yes," she said. "Geminis."

"Why don't I take you there for dinner," he said. "To thank you for all you've done for me."

She knew it would bring her only trouble. Still, she couldn't fight the desire to rebel against her own instincts. As easily as slipping a needle under her skin, she heard herself saying yes.

Tiphaine seemed lost in thought as she negotiated the dangerous curves of the road that led to Santa Rosa, her hands vibrating on the steering wheel, a cigarette between her fingers. Bordered by the ocean on one side and trees on the other, it was the only paved throughway that led to the town. Austin had heard that tourists were regularly robbed on this road by thieves pretending to have a flat tire or placed pylons on the road and then, armed with machetes, jumped lazily from the bushes.

They had just passed a rare building, a lone pharmacy open late, when Tiphane suddenly slammed on the brakes to avoid hitting an iguana.

"Nearly a goodbye party," she said, putting the car back into gear.

All week Austin had imagined what he would say to Tiphaine during the drive. Yet all he could focus on now was the hard line of her jaw, her cupid lips, and the glint in her eye as dangerous as the flash of a knife, and how even so, he couldn't imagine a single man on earth who wouldn't do anything for her. He was reminded of the policemen he'd seen talking to her in the evenings when he was emptying out the garbage cans. Whatever she said to them, they always left her and her altered books alone when even the cooks knew what she did to those tabs. It was possible that no one had ever complained. But he wondered about luck and when hers would run out.

"The thing that's different about us is that you can leave whenever you want," she said, as if sharing only the tail end of a conversation she was having with herself.

"But why would I want to? So I can go home and get some nine-to-five job I have to wear a suit and tie for? No thanks."

"I think you look at my life and think it's all fun and games."

"What's wrong with having fun in life?"

She shot him a condescending glance as she took another drag of her cigarette.

"Life's what you make of it. I mean, it's not rocket science." He stared out the window at the water and the dying sun, questioning for the first time just how she'd made it this far.

When they arrived at Geminis, they parked under some coconut trees and passed a mountain of split-open husks crawling with geckos. They walked toward a nearby plaza where a Mariachi band was playing and dancing couples glided between stone benches, their shadows long and graceful in the setting sun. In less than half an hour the sky would be black. The speed with which night swallowed day still amazed Tiphaine; only in the tropics could something change its nature so quickly. As they strolled along the wooden pier that led to the restaurant, they took off their shoes; the pier's boards were still hot beneath their feet. Rocking fish boats and the children playing on the boardwalk were silhouetted against the sunset's glow.

As they neared the restaurant, Austin motioned toward the sand. At first she wasn't sure what he was pointing at, but then the fading light reflecting off the ocean cast an orange shimmer onto the figures.

Two figures.

Their faces drifted toward each other, closing the space the sun's dying rays had formed between them as Chato pulled the Dutch girl Marie into him for a deep kiss.

Tiphaine grabbed the sea wall in front of her and felt a shifting in her bones, a settling – and then nothing. She watched the two figures until the clouds rolled in and it started to rain, streaks striping the sky. Then Chato and Marie joined the other people caught in the downpour who ran under store awnings and held newspapers over their heads, laughing and crowding against one another.

Back in the safety of the car, Austin silent beside her, Tiphaine sat smoking and holding her hands, the one thing she could do, while the palm trees outside bucked under the weight of the rain. The trembling rose from deep within her until her shoulders were shaking, too. The image of Chato and Marie flashed in her mind, their faces turned up to the rain, and Marie opening out her arms to him.

If she'd been alone Tiphaine might have marched up to them, grabbed Marie by her hair and shoved her face into the sand. Or driven back to El Principe and burned the place down. Or told Chato she was leaving, going back to Paris.

Run. That's all she wanted to do. And take her son with her.

Instead, she threw her cigarette out the window and fixed her makeup in the rearview mirror. "So?" she said at last. "What are you going to order when we get inside?"

When Marie returned from the beach the next day, she discovered her hammock and backpack missing from the luggage loft.

"Your things have been confiscated," Tiphaine told her.

"Confiscated?"

"You owe one week of back rent on your hammock space."

Chato and Austin glanced up from the wooden table where they sat playing cards as usual. Austin guzzled from his beer, afraid to meet Tiphaine's eyes. Chato leaned back in his chair and spit onto the ground. Even the cooks behind Tiphaine stopped gossiping as Marie replied that she put money on her bill every third day. "There's no way I owe you that much."

"Your backpack has been confiscated," Tiphaine said again, her eyes unblinking. "I give people credit out of kindness. But this is also a business. When the bill is so high, and you won't pay, there is nothing I can do."

Marie made her own calculations and barked that she would pay this much and not a penny more.

Tiphaine shook her head. Then she calmly picked up the debt book, folded it under her arm, and went into the kitchen.

Marie looked at Chato. "Aren't you going to do something?"

Chato shrugged.

"I'll go to the police," Marie yelled at Tiphaine's back.

"And I will show them these records," Tiphaine called over her shoulder. "You think I don't already know every policeman here?"

Kirstie, who had been hanging her bathing suit to dry on the fence, now stood beside her sister at the counter. She took Marie's elbow and tried to pull her away, which only enraged her further.

"I'm not going to stand for it! Do you think I'll put up with this kind of treatment?" Marie glared at Chato as she walked over to his table and stood there, her feet planted in the sand.

Chato put his hands behind his head and raised his eyebrows as if to say, What can I do? He shook his head again. "Let me tell you about Tiphaine," he said, staring drunkenly. "She's *loca*, crazy. Pay her. That is the best thing to do."

Marie flicked her cigarette at the sand by his feet.

"Forget it," Kirstie said again, touching Marie's arm. "Let's just go."

But Marie was not going to give up. She and her sister took a *colectivo* to the police station, sitting together in the front seat, sweat pooling under their thighs because of the plastic seat covers, the air from the back window sucked up by a pregnant woman on one side and two kids bouncing up and down in their school uniforms on the other.

At the station, Marie told the *commandante* that the owners of El Principe were cheating their customers, selling drugs, and running a brothel. Her sister could confirm the one and she could tell him where to look for the other.

The *commandante* shook his head sadly, frustrated by these demanding tourist-types. Twenty years ago, none of these resorts had existed. Now they jutted out like broken limbs on every sheet of sand.

"Unless you take my complaint of fraud and everything else I've told you about seriously, I'm not leaving," Marie said.

The *commandante* could only sigh as he went to fetch his logbook.

That evening, the police marched through the bamboo gate of El Principe. They were smiling, jovial, as always, but something about their shiny black leather boots and machine guns seemed more threatening than usual, as though gleaming with some kind of truth.

Near the last hammock at the back of the *palapa* hut, Austin stood as still as he possibly could, not wanting to draw attention to himself. With the least amount of motion he could manage, he fumbled with the plastic straws filled with coke he kept in the front pocket of his cutoff shorts and dropped the straws to the ground. Then, with his foot, he covered the powder and the straws with sand. The police couldn't arrest him if he had nothing incriminating in his possession. When he looked up again to take in the commotion of lights crashing and glass shattering as the police tore apart the resort with terrible efficiency, he thought maybe he'd made a mistake staying in Cayo Bonaire for as long as he had. If he didn't get arrested and thrown into a Central American prison, he swore to himself he'd fly home as soon as he could.

The police had Chato against the wall. He raised his eyebrows, threw out his hands, and shrugged in the casual way of someone who has nothing to hide. On the other side of the *palapa* hut, an officer was speaking to Tiphaine, her eyes cast down.

Before, she'd always seemed so out of his reach. Austin knew he was being selfish, wanting to see her break, but she'd wounded him and no one should be allowed that kind of power. Now it appeared as though Tiphaine's luck had finally run out. The police were taking the place apart.

One of the officers pointed at Austin with his machine gun, grinning in a mocking way as he said something to make his partner laugh. *El gabacho mas guacho.* Hustler. Austin wiped his lips with his hand as he worried about whether they would question him, but they continued their search. When they found a quarter-pound of Chato's personal redhair rolled into a newspaper under the large cooler in the kitchen, filled with beer, they hesitated, looking almost apologetically at Chato and Tiphaine. The police didn't even bother with the handcuffs as they led Chato and

Tiphaine across the sand toward the police car parked in the street, where kids had stopped their baseball game to peer through the fence at what was happening.

"Find Olivia," Tipahine said to Austin as they passed him, the desperation clear in her voice. "She has to tell Luz what's happened. And Sebastian —" But she couldn't bring herself to finish her sentence.

"*M'ijo,*" Chato said, calling out for Austin. "I'll call you when I know about the fine."

But Austin knew Chato and Tiphaine didn't have any money. Whatever hadn't gone up her nose, Chato had spent on women; any amount would be too much.

That night and all of the next day, Austin waited by the phone at El Principe, his bag packed for Arizona and waiting by his side. When the phone finally rang, he found it hard to breathe, the fear catching in his throat. His hand trembled when he picked up the receiver. What could he say to Tiphaine to comfort her?

She told him about the heat in the cells, the bedbugs. Each word was a thin, unsteady soprano more whispered than spoken, airy as a desert and just as empty. "I, I don't know about things anymore," she said.

"How much does he want?"

"He wants too much."

The words barbed his heart and wouldn't let go. They made him wonder how things could have been different. If she was rid of Chato and free of all that madness. If she kept herself clean. He could have kept her happy, could have kept her and Sebastian safe. And maybe if he stayed in Honduras just a little longer, he still could.

As Tiphaine listened to Austin reassure her that he would ask his parents for a loan or offer the *commandante* information in exchange for her freedom, she thought back to being with Chato in the police car. How he'd turned to her across the back seat, looking at her with confusion the way he had once before, when he'd caught her snorting his personal stash. She knew he'd wanted to shout at her, but, instead, he'd touched her lips with his fingers and said nothing. Just gazed at her, his eyes so strange then, as if he were trying to slice her open, to discover what part of her was still his and what part he had lost. A person will grab anything to stop himself from falling, Tiphaine had thought, even the edge of a knife.

It wasn't catching him with Marie that made her do what she did next. Tiphaine's love for Chato was too much for one person to bear; she'd never been able to carry its weight. Maybe you had to push yourself away from a love like that. And Sebastian, her beautiful boy, he didn't need her falling; her getting up only to fall back down again. He was still young enough to forget and to move on without them.

She told Austin what he already suspected: "There is no money. The *commandante* wants $5,000 American and there is no money."

"I'll do what I can."

"No," she said. "Don't."

"Thank you," Herr Müller said, as Elke poured coffee into his cup. "It smells good and strong."

Elke smoothed her hands over her starched white apron before taking it off and folding it over the back of her chair — proud she'd passed this test, made coffee the way his wife would make it. She felt her cheeks flush, so she lowered her gaze and let it settle on the braided rug on the kitchen floor.

"You don't always have to wear your uniform," Herr Müller said. "You could wear some of my wife's clothes. She's the same size as you."

Joachim groaned.

"Mama has pretty dresses," Daniel said. "My favourite is the one with swirls."

"What do you know?" Berbyl said.

When Elke first arrived at the Müller farm, she had expected babies she could carry like baskets and toddlers who'd cling to her shirt, not this: Daniel, five and feral, with elderberry twigs in his hair and pockets she had to empty nightly of feathers and dead beetles; and Berbyl, who was twelve, surly, and standoffish. How many times had Elke tried to draw the girl out of her room, where she sat all day playing with paper cut-outs of maids and kings she had drawn herself?

Then there was fifteen-year-old Joachim. Only four years younger than Elke, he was raw boned and sharp-eyed and clutched his fork with large, awkward hands he had not yet grown into, though he seemed emboldened by their new size. His brown sloping gaze made her skin burn, as if he could see through her uniform — all her nerves torn loose beneath. He had his father's eyes, and they reminded her of the eyes on the deer Herr Müller's wife had painted on the china plates decorating the buffet.

"Why does *she* get everything?" Berbyl yelled suddenly.

Herr Müller flashed his daughter a withering glance.

"It's not fair, why don't *I* get letters?"

"You need to write letters to get letters," he said. "Who do you write letters to?"

"But I don't care about that!"

Elke gripped the edge of her seat.

"Go to your room." Herr Müller's voice sounded strained by the effort to keep it steady.

Berbyl glared at her father as she got up from the table and scraped her chair across the floor. As she walked past Elke she leaned over and hissed into her ear, "You'd look worse than *anyone* in Mama's dresses."

The day Elke had arrived on the farm, Berbyl circled the room they'd newly made up for her — fresh slivers still ringed the screw holes around the hasp latch Herr Müller had put on the door for Elke's benefit. Elke felt bad for Berbyl. Under her overalls, her body was already pear-shaped. And such thick glasses! Maybe she could braid the girl's hair. They could talk and share secrets the way she and her sisters did.

"What a room!" Berbyl had said. "I'd like to sleep in here sometimes, can I?"

"Let our visitor get settled," her father said. "Come, Berbyl."

"It's okay," Elke said. "She can help me unpack."

After her father left, Berbyl sat at the edge of the bed, her feet dangling above the floor.

Elke moved the frame with Da-Nhât's picture to make room for her hairbrush and hand mirror on the night stand. "Do you have a boyfriend?" Elke asked. Then she wondered if it was unprofessional to ask so personal a question.

"All the boys in my class like Annette Schnorr, because her mother makes nice cookies, and she's very kind. It doesn't matter. I just eat my lunch alone."

Elke pictured her on a bench, head down, stones at her feet. Her next question would be more professional. "You must have friends?"

Berbyl shrugged. "Not really. No one likes the games I play."

"What kind of games do you play?"

"I like to pretend. I like to play pretend games."

Berbyl was nothing like Elke's own sisters. For Berbyl, being sent to her room was more relief than punishment.

She was just a child, prone to tantrums at that, but not for the first time Elke wondered how different the children were when their mother was around.

"Who's the letter from?" Joachim asked, interrupting Elke's thoughts. "Your boyfriend?"

A letter? Perhaps from Da-Nhât to ask why she hadn't yet responded to his proposal. She'd sent him a letter a few days ago – surely it hadn't already arrived.

Herr Müller shook his head in reprimand at Joachim. "Yes, right. After lunch. Don't let me forget to give it to you. It came today."

Joachim speared two more sausages from the serving dish. A lock of hair fell over one eye as he looked at his father. "You realize you ask Elke about Mama's clothes every single day."

Herr Müller chuckled nervously. "Not to give," he said. "To borrow."

"My uniform is fine," Elke said. She'd been tempted to say yes to Herr Müller's offer every day these three weeks she'd been at the farm, because she owned only two dresses of her own that were not handed down from a sister.

"Mama and you are not the same size," Daniel piped in. "Mama's tummy is fatter. She has a baby growing in there."

Herr Müller smiled sadly as he rumpled Daniel's hair. "You miss Mama, don't you?"

She was about to ask Daniel whether he wanted a baby brother or sister, but stopped because she wasn't supposed to discuss private matters with the family – such a question might be seen as too intimate. She hadn't even been told the details of Frau Müller's convalescence.

"I don't miss Mama," Daniel said. "I like Elke. She has long eyelashes."

Every night Daniel would cry for his mother, and every night she would stroke his cocoon-white hair and sing "Sleep Child Sleep" until he drifted off. Later, as she tiptoed out of Daniel's room so the wooden floorboards wouldn't creak, Elke's stomach would flutter as she recalled how a state employee named Ute had once filled her own mother's absence in her family's home like a prosthetic limb, after her mother had the cancer in her ovaries removed. She'd forgotten whether her mother had gone to the convalescence spa in Schandau or Marienburg or Tölz, but she remembered how, when they were alone, Ute would speak to her almost like a sister.

Now Elke was such a worker. Someone to rock Daniel to sleep, wash the family clothes, cook, clean, and take her place opposite Herr Müller at the table, sitting in his wife's chair.

After they finished eating, Joachim watched Elke clear the dishes, patting his lips with the cloth napkin she'd ironed that morning. He placed the napkin on the table then cracked his knuckles, trying to discomfort her.

The first day, Joachim had come to her room with his father to see how she was settling in. Joachim held a feather blanket in his arms.

As she thanked him and placed the blanket at the foot of her bed, Herr Müller noticed the pictures she'd brought from home: one of John F. Kennedy that hung on the wall, one of Jesus, and on the nightstand, in a small black frame, one of Da-Nhât sitting astride his Lambretta scooter in front of the business building at the Sorbonne, wearing a slim tie and a suit with narrow lapels, his hair wavy and pomaded so that he looked like the French New Wave actor Jean-Paul Belmondo.

Joachim had leaned over to take a closer look at the photo. "Nice bike."

Continuing to unpack, she told them about how she had met Da-Nhât through a magazine for pen pals, and how they were learning English together. How he lived in Paris now, but had lived everywhere. How he was from Vietnam and very avant-garde, and how one day they might even get married and move to America.

When she had stopped talking, Herr Müller raised his eyebrows, a grin playing about his lips. On the surface, Joachim's smile didn't change, but there was a tension in the skin of his forehead, a minute tightening in his jaw. He pulled his earlobe and stared at an imaginary spot past her shoulder, unable to meet her gaze. Moments in which no one said a word ticked by, until the silence was finally broken by the crack of Joachim's knuckles.

Now Joachim again cracked his knuckles while she dropped dirty plates into the soapy dish water.

Though her back was to him, she could feel Joachim's eyes tracking her movements and, imagining them, she became so flustered she almost dropped a cup. A swirl of coffee floated to the surface of the water and then vanished. What was she doing?

Not until Herr Müller brought her the letter he'd mentioned did she realize she'd forgotten to put her apron back on. There was gravy spattered down the front of her uniform;

she'd have to scrub it and hope it would be dry enough to wear in the morning.

She rubbed the plates with a cloth and tried to picture herself somewhere else, ordering dinner at a restaurant in New York, maybe, with her hair done up in a chignon and silk stockings on her feet. In America. The word melted in her mouth like chocolate.

As soon as she was finished with the dishes, she hurried to her room to read the letter. She could see Herr Müller from her window walking toward the barn, Joachim and Daniel flagging behind, tossing the cat back and forth like a sack of flour between them.

Elke's room was next to the storage shed, where she imagined potatoes grew eyes in the dark while the apples softened. Reaching for the letter in her apron, she noticed the key to her padlock was missing. She was sure she had left it in her apron's front pocket.

Being unable to lock herself in for privacy unsettled her, not that she believed someone would intrude, but because the lock and its key reminded her of how she'd felt in Da-Nhât's hotel room that first time. Away from the noise of the two-bedroom apartment she shared with her parents and five siblings, with a place to finally call her own.

She had bought the lock shortly after she'd arrived at the Müllers'. Joachim had knocked on her door and leaned against the doorframe, his arm blocking the threshold. He hadn't spoken two words to her since she'd arrived, and now he stood peering past her into her bedroom.

"My father's having a friend over and they'll be drinking tonight," he said, "You'd better stay in here."

The way his hand was planted on the doorframe, his shadow falling across the floor of her room, suddenly made her wish she was back home in Rendsburg.

All through her training at the Evangelical School for Home Care, she'd yearned for a posting with her own room. Now she missed the crowded apartment, and her family, and the drab, factory-smogged, military-barracked city – even the loathsome market where she shopped for groceries week in and week out, with its buckets of churning eels stinking in the rain.

That night Herr Müller and his friend had pounded their beer steins on the table, singing like alley cats, their voices rising and falling where they pleased, "Thoughts are free, who can guess them? No man can know them, no hunter can shoot them."

The next day she'd walked into town and bought a fashion magazine, a chocolate bar, and a padlock from the hardware store.

No one, not even Herr Müller, knew she had the lock. But now the key was gone.

With nothing to be done about the missing key for now, she pulled the letter from her apron and was disappointed to see the letter was postmarked Rendsburg. It wasn't from Da-Nhât, but from her mother.

Along with news about how her brother Gerhard had managed his janitorial exams, her mother had sent her the Evangelical School's new brochure, which included a photograph of her leaning studiously over a table full of books and binders. How ridiculous. She'd been the least academic of all the students, always afraid a teacher would cross-examine her, doubting her own intellect.

In the last letter she had received from Da-Nhât before leaving for the Müller farm, he had written, "How interesting my friends in Vietnam would think me to be, to have a German banking position and a German wife." Was it a proposal? She'd looked up nearly every word of his letter in a German-English dictionary, but she still couldn't be sure.

She slumped further down on her cot and ran her hands over the duck-down blanket. John F. Kennedy stared at her from the wall. She'd fallen in love with him when he said the words, "*Ich bin ein Berliner,*" and she had cried for two weeks when he died, even though she wasn't political. In fact, she was awed by students like those demonstrating in Paris. They knew things she didn't. She knew small things: how rain fell on a North Sea wave; how her mother looked when she wore her blue suit to church, her waist as trim as a paintbrush; how a purple fig tasted when plucked, encrusted in sugar, from a vendor's cart in the evening.

"Do you know they gave me the best blanket in the house?"

JFK nodded and said, "I know."

She turned from JFK to her picture of Jesus. "I'm a selfish girl, aren't I? And I miss my mother."

After putting her mother's letter under her pillow, Elke walked down the hall to Herr Müller's bedroom to dust and polish, as she did every day. The room was spare but tidy: an armoire, a chest of drawers, a bed with a handmade spread, a dresser with an oval mirror, on top of which stood a basin and a pitcher decorated with the same deer painted on the china in the kitchen.

The wooden crib that usually stood by the bed had been moved to beneath the window, and there were two woollen socks and a pair of work pants hanging from the railing. She suspected Herr Müller had pushed it against the wall to make more space for himself until his wife came home. Yesterday, she had plucked two well-thumbed Goethe books from where they rested on the white eyelet cover. Yes, the family needed her to keep things tidy until the baby arrived. She picked up the socks and pants and put them by the door to wash later.

As she dusted, she hummed a song, her thoughts circling around to Herr Müller's wife, Sigrid. Did she sing while she worked? Were they Pentecostal hymns like the ones Elke sang or Catholic ones? Did Catholics sing? Elke wondered.

She dusted the crib railings and smoothed the quilt; she dusted the mirror of the dresser, then its wooden surface. On the dresser sat a small soapbox. She held it to her nose and breathed in the scent of flowers, dying and sweet. Was this the scent that lingered in the air by the sink when Sigrid was home?

She opened the box and saw a hat pin, a silver broach, a heart-shaped pendant, and four pairs of earrings, clip-ons and pierced. No one Elke knew had pierced ears. Her mother said earrings were for Jezebels.

Elke held a pair of pearl-drop earrings to her face and marvelled at how they caught the sunlight. She clipped on one and then the other, stroking her hair behind her ears to get a better look at herself in the mirror, wondering if she looked like a Parisian woman. Then she noticed something else at the bottom of the soap box; she'd seen her brother use cigarette papers before, but these were pink.

She closed up the soap box, picked up the rag and the bottle of wood oil. As she ran the cloth over the scratched wooden surface of the armoire, she realized she had never looked inside before because she'd always been so sure of what she would find: suits like her mother's, work clothes for cleaning, dresses shaped like duffel bags, and snoods to cover hair that had been set in pin curls no matter how much her mother's fingers ached from scrubbing, because to do otherwise would make her no better than "a common Turkish cleaning woman."

The wardrobe door creaked as she opened it. She noticed a blue suit jacket first and brushed the dust off its shoulders. The boys' distant voices carried through the open window, wafting in on a breeze that smelled tangy with manure. She held her fingers on the shoulder of the coat, letting them linger there, imagining the man outside with the cows and milking machine as a whole other man, inside this jacket, with Sigrid here in this bedroom.

One of the dresses was red with pearl buttons. The suppleness of the brightly coloured silk between her thumb and forefinger surprised her. She had pictured Sigrid in dreary wool, like every woman she'd ever known. She pulled the dress from the wardrobe and held the red fabric against her chest, twirling a little to see how the skirt flared.

"There you are."

Herr Müller stood in the doorway of the bedroom, his frame blocking much of the light that streamed down the hall, casting his face in shadow as he took a step toward her. She imagined he might touch her body. Instead he reached out and flicked lightly at the earrings.

"Those earrings look very nice on you," he said, smiling. "Do you think your boyfriend would like you wearing them?" He let his hand drop.

"I have work to do," she said, quickly hanging the dress back on the wooden rod. "I was just dusting."

"Go on then." He chuckled, crossed his arms, and turned his body, as if to let her pass by, but did not move from where he stood. As he shifted his weight, a shaft of sunshine fell across his shirt and over his forearms, as thick and brown as loaves of bread. At the base of each hair was a golden freckle.

"This boyfriend of yours," he said. "He will be trouble for you."

In alarm, she sat down on the bed. To prove she wasn't scared, she looked up and held his gaze. "I know how to handle myself."

"I know that, I know." He sat down next to her. He paused for a moment. "But it's complicated."

She ran her hand over the quilted triangles of the spread. "I don't know what you mean."

"He's not like us. People can be, so — unaccepting."

She remembered walking from the train station with Da-Nhât that day in Hamburg, how a mother had made a small *tschick* noise with her tongue and hurried her children up the street as she noticed Elke holding his hand, and how, by contrast, an Albanian grocery store clerk had gazed toward Da-Nhât, then at Elke and her brother before looking at Da-Nhât again and grinning with surprise and admiration – and a kind of hunger.

She knew that even outside Rendsburg, there were few foreigners living in Germany. Those who married Germans were still considered foreigners. Their children, too. She knew Hamburg: the harness races at the Trabrennbahn, the Altona, and the pretty Elbe, the harbour with its tiered promenades and tall ships. How many foreigners had she ever seen on the promenade? And how much *Ausländer raus*, "foreigner out" graffiti? She recalled a newspaper article about a Turkish tulip seller from the Grosse Elbstrasse market who was followed from a nightclub by a group of teenagers on Goebbels's birthday. He had been left unconscious and bleeding, his delivery truck set aflame.

"Are you cold?" he said.

She shook her head.

"You're so slim. You should eat more."

She imagined him moving closer. Pushing her down onto the bed with his palm flat against her chest. His hand moving over the buttons of her blouse. She imagined crying out. His lips solidly halting her exclamation. But he stood up and ran his fingers through his hair. At the door he turned and gave her a lopsided smile.

As soon as he was gone, she yanked the earrings off so hard her skin burned.

A month before she left for Herr Müller's farm, Da-Nhât had visited her for the first time. They'd been corresponding for seven months, ever since she'd seen Da-Nhât's passport-sized photograph in a pen-pal magazine over the caption, "Seeking English-speaking partner." She didn't speak English, but admiring his photo she was reminded of how she'd always wanted to learn.

He was ten years older and she could imagine him sitting at outdoor cafés with sophisticated women who wore gold sandals and could talk about art films and exhale cigarette smoke through their noses like dragons.

Elke and her older brother Peter had met Da-Nhât at the train station in Hamburg, a city eighty kilometres south of Rendsburg. His designer clothing oozed Parisian chic. She'd never seen hair so black, or so thick. She was tempted to reach out and wind her fingers through his pomaded waves – would they feel hot from the sun like black stones in the summer? She touched her own hair then, usually plaited into two girlish braids her mother tightened for her every day, but which she had spent the morning teasing into a beehive instead.

"Hello, Elke? Peter? I am happy to see you," Da-Nhât said in enunciated German. His face broke open into a grin when he shook their hands and bowed.

"Wo-ow," Peter said, eager to practise what little English he'd learned during his first year of youth military service. "You are speak German."

Elke had been studying English language cassettes she'd asked her brother to buy for her while he was in Kiel.

"Hello," she said, feeling silly and self-conscious. "I am pleased to meet you."

Da-Nhât pressed her hand between his.

"Can we go shopping?" He held out a piece of paper.

"What for?" she asked. "What are these things?"

He explained in English only slightly less broken than his German that it was a grocery list he had prepared on the train. "For cooking," he said.

Peter laughed and said in German, "You're not planning on making lunch, are you?"

"You will see," he said. "You will see."

Garlic? Tamarind sauce? Heaven knew if the things on his list even existed. Elke hadn't heard of half of them. She was all the more surprised when Da-Nhât succeeded in obtaining them in the third grocery they visited.

The ride back was peppered with conversation about family; Elke told Da-Nhât about their cocker spaniel and the feral one-eyed alley cat they called Morley and left their food scraps for on the fire escape. Beyond the car windows, inner-city buildings changed to factories, then farms, and by the time they reached the family's apartment building on Prinzessinstrasse, back to brick again.

While Elke set the table, she watched her mother hovering over Da-Nhât in the kitchen, asking him the names of each dish and inquiring where he had learned to cook. Elke could hear the twins squealing outside in the courtyard and the sound of a rubber ball hitting a wall. Both sets of voices wafted into the room where they'd set up the table, and mingled in what Elke hoped was a harmonious way.

Though there was still a high pitch to her mother's voice, she seemed more relaxed than when Da-Nhât had first arrived. Through the kitchen door, Elke listened to her mother's questions about this spice or that marinade and Da-Nhât's answers about their exotic ports of origin.

"That one looks strange," she heard her mother say. "What does it taste like?"

"Oh," he said. "This one taste very sweet. Very good."

An unusually long pause made Elke look up. Da-Nhât was holding out his hand, his finger covered in a thick sauce the colour of clotted blood. Her mother looked at Da-Nhât, a spoon in her hand, her lips pursed into the shape of a small, tight bud. A breeze blew in and rippled the table cloth against Elke's leg. No one spoke. Then her mother opened her mouth and licked his finger.

"*Gut!*" she pronounced.

She went back to chattering about her own cooking and Da-Nhât wiped his finger clean on a kitchen towel and, just like that, the rift that had opened up for an instant closed again.

Later, Elke's father sat down at the head of the table in his nicest slacks, coughing. He was a man who took pride in clean white shirts, collars that were always pressed, and wearing silk ties on weekdays. He had contracted tuberculosis in the Russian mud before Elke was born, during the war. Afterwards, the military hospital had sawed open his sternum, renting his body wide, and removed one of his lungs. The operation had left him with a hollow space in his chest as large as a child's fist, which he hid under impeccably maintained clothes, shamed by his disfigurement.

But sometimes her father would let her touch the scar. As small children, she and her siblings had lined up at their father's bedside to place their palms in the hollow, giggling as their flesh was swallowed up by his. She would feel his heart beating, and touch the expansion of his breath where he'd been cracked open, until finally, in exasperation, he shooed them away.

As he continued to cough, Elke stared at the grandfather clock, at the roses carved into the wood, the anchor, the rooster. There were two clocks in every room. *Tick-tock*, like her father's coughing. Her father tried to say grace, and while they waited for the coughing to subside, her mother rested her hand over top of his. Finally, he finished giving thanks, and everyone said, "Amen."

Elke had not looked at anyone's face as she helped Da-Nhât bring out the food from the kitchen: greasy cigar-sized rolls with wrinkled skin through which shredded carrot shone, cucumbers with a black sauce, pancakes the size of dinner plates, a whole fish with the eyes still in its head! Now she studied the expressions of her parents, who were eating with small, polite bites, but her mother's face was a mask Elke couldn't read. Under the table, the twins fed the cocker spaniel. Her father, drinking more than eating, questioned Da-Nhât on matters of education, family, and ambition, while the twins giggled and her older sisters elbowed each other.

"Tomorrow I will go to Hamburg for job interview at bank. I like Hamburg. Nice city. Job at bank will be good, very good. I am glad to be able to stop here, visit Elke on the way."

"You've applied for a job in Hamburg?" her father asked. "Why Hamburg?"

"To be close to my Elke."

Her father coughed and looked into his beer.

Her mother laughed and hid another piece of food in her apron.

"You know," Da-Nhât lowered his voice, "in my country, when the moon is full my people go outside to write poem. Play chess. Sit under its light. The Vietnamese say the moon is full with blond-haired womens, beautiful, like your daughter, and that is why it is so bright. It is where all the blond-haired people live and why all the young men dreams about it. My ex-girlfriend was dark hair, the daughter of the French ambassador to Iraq, rich with too many parties in her apartment on the Champs Elysées. Drugs. Bah." He shook his head. "Not like Elke."

How could he speak so openly, without a hint of embarrassment or reserve? Was it Paris that made men this way?

He touched her hand across the table. Her sisters blushed. The twins snickered some more. Her father coughed.

"What are you studying at the Sorbonne?" her mother asked, giving the twins an admonishing glance.

"Business."

"Your mother must miss you terribly."

"My parents want me to travel. Even before war. In my country, the bombs destroy beautiful temple, art."

"Is that why you left? The war?" her father asked.

Da-Nhât shook his head.

What was it like, Elke wondered, to leave a whole life behind the way a snake sheds its skin? Did Da-Nhât feel free?

"I'd like to travel," Elke said. "In Rendsburg, the farthest people travel is a daytrip to the North Sea for picnics. Once, a teacher of mine went to Tunisia for two weeks. Of course, that's not the same, really."

"Good adventure."

She raised her glass and took a drink.

"I am happy," Da-Nhât said, emphasizing his words with his own personal pair of chopsticks, "to meet you all." He plucked the fish eye from the head of the cod; then, to their amazement, and her mother's obvious disgust, he swallowed it whole, looking as satisfied as if he'd swallowed the moon.

Elke was beating a rug on the front step when she heard car tires crunch to a stop beyond the hedgerow fence. She heard a voice ask for directions from the neighbouring farmer who had been walking down the road.

"Elke Schröder? The Müllers?"

The farmer answered he knew of no such people.

The lilting rise and fall of his syllables had always reminded her of a galloping horse. She dropped the rug and ran to the road. "Da-Nhât!"

As Da-Nhât stepped out of his car, the farmer grunted and smoothed his beard before turning away. Still holding the stick she'd used to beat the rug, she threw her arms around him, and in her excitement, hit his head with her own. She pulled away at precisely the same moment he hugged her back, a jerky push-pull of movement that made her self-conscious, and the words that followed came out hesitant and faltering.

"I look for you one hour," he said, surveying her at an arm's length.

"How long can you stay?" she said, looking straight into his eyes. She had remembered him as much taller.

"I can stay until evening then I must leave again. I lose much time because no one tells me where you are. I have to stop at four farms."

She glanced around. Herr Müller would soon come out of the house.

"I was at bank in Hamburg this morning."

Out of the corner of her eye she thought she saw a curtain flutter.

"Then I go see your mother. But she not gives me the address."

"You didn't get my letter?"

Their exchange, in English and German, was similar to their hug, stop-and-go.

When she turned around again, Herr Müller had come out into the yard, Joachim following two paces behind him, while Daniel stood by the door of the house.

"Herr Müller, this is Da-Nhât Nguyen," she said, hoping she had pronounced it correctly. *Nya-Nyuck Wen.* She had practised it over and over, after he'd corrected her, much to her embarrassment, at the train station.

"Yes, I *know.*" Herr Müller grinned at Da-Nhât and they shook hands, Herr Müller as stocky and platinum-haired as Da-Nhât was lissome and dark.

"Where are you from?" Daniel asked, moving aside on the threshold. "Do you like airplanes?" He was already holding his favourite fighters and bombers. When Da-Nhât responded yes, Daniel said, "This is a Messerschmitt. *Brrrrrrrrrrr.*" He flew the plane across Da-Nhât's path as Herr Müller steered him inside.

Joachim nodded coolly at Da-Nhât, looking through him in that way of his, fathoming the possibilities. He trudged behind his father, maybe resentfully, as Herr Müller placed one hand behind Da-Nhât's back to guide him. Elke followed them into the kitchen, where Herr Müller set down a beer in front of Da-Nhât.

Elke began to prepare lunch, her jaw tense, as she peeled the skins off the boiled potatoes. Daniel played at the table with his chair pulled close to Da-Nhât's. Running a tank over Da-Nhât's place mat, he knocked Da-Nhât's fork to the floor. Da-Nhât picked it up and skimmed it over Daniel's arm, making the noise of an airplane.

"Berbyl," Herr Müller called, "we have a guest. Come out of your room and be polite."

She emerged holding a dirty stuffed cat. "This is Cream Puff," she said, letting Da-Nhât pet its matted fur. "Watch out. She bites." Berbyl pulled the toy back. "Cream Puff is a little sensitive, right here, around the ears." Then she reached out and touched Da-Nhât's hair. "Eew. It feels like a Brillo Pad."

"Berbyl," Elke said, "sit down!"

She sat down, seesawing in her chair. "Is lunch ready?"

"Not yet," Elke said.

"Now?"

Daniel retrieved some colouring pencils from his room and asked Da-Nhât if he knew how to draw a Panzer.

"Elke tells me you're studying business," Herr Müller said.

While the men talked, Elke brought the food to the table. "Toys off the table, Berbyl."

"Not Cream Puff. She wants sausages."

"She can eat yours."

"So she can stay?"

"I have thirty-seven cows and two milking machines," Herr Müller continued. "If you like, I'll show them to you after lunch."

"I hate milk," Berbyl said.

"Berbyl," Elke said, pointing at the filthy toy next to Berbyl's plate. "Cat."

"It's not fair. Daniel has a pencil at the table."

"You should see the milking machines," Elke said to Da-Nhât. "They're quite new."

"I like very much," Da-Nhât said.

Herr Müller laughed and slapped Da-Nhât on the back.

Joachim still hadn't said a word; he'd shovelled in his food, and now he was drumming his fingers on the table, pretending to be interested in the view out the window. Finally he said, "You like music?"

"Oh, yes, very good. Paris has the most romance music in the world. And movies. You know Brigitte Bardot? She is my favourite actress."

"What do you think of the foreign occupation of Vietnam?" Herr Müller asked Da-Nhât.

"The fighting. It is terrible what it is doing to my country."

"Are you a soldier?" Berbyl said.

"I've heard about the demonstrations in Paris," Joachim said. "All the students in the streets."

"Young people have rights. The right not to lose everything. The future belong to them."

"And what about the old?" Herr Müller asked.

"Old have rights, too. But young people are future." Da-Nhât looked at Berbyl. "You're right. War is very bad."

Elke gave Herr Müller another beer. "I always ask Elke if she has enough clothes," he said, "because she could wear my wife's. They are the same size."

Elke turned her gaze to Da-Nhât, unsure of how he would react – she had never seen him angry before – but he just nodded. She could feel her cheeks burn as she continued to smile.

"That dishes are very beautiful," Da-Nhât said, pointing with his knife to the china on the buffet.

"Sigrid painted those," Herr Müller said.

"So beautiful. Will your wife be joining you soon?" The smile dropped from Herr Müller's face. Berbyl and Joachim both looked away. Elke couldn't believe he had tossed the question into the air as casually as if Sigrid were merely making tea in the next room. She was suddenly ashamed for all the times she herself had wondered when Sigrid would return. No one she knew would ever ask such a personal question, force open a space that had never been open before.

"Sigrid is recovering," Herr Müller replied quietly. "Our baby was stillborn."

After lunch Da-Nhât asked Elke if he could accompany her as she fetched the cows from the far field. She nodded, heartened by his excitement, and they set off down the road holding hands, his backpack bouncing on his shoulders. Yet her own thoughts kept returning to Herr Müller, the way he'd risen from his chair at lunch, placed his fingers on the wooden table, and turned to look at Da-Nhât, a strain in each word as he said, "It's been a real pleasure." Something in the room had cracked open, and she thought she heard a sound like a stream of air rushing into a vacuum.

"How do you get the cows to follow you?" Da-Nhât asked.

"Hmmm? Oh, it's easy."

"Do you whistle?"

"If they fall behind, you hit them a little on the rump with a stick. But they know where the barn is. They mostly come on their own."

They walked on and the sun moved lower in the sky, hanging above the thatch-roofed houses where storks rested. Da-Nhât picked up a stone and tossed it into the air again and again. "How are the Müllers? Are they treat you nice?"

"They're a good family." She laughed and touched his shoulder. "Why? Were you worried about me? You were, weren't you?" She felt her cheeks flush and was grateful for the cool wind. She loved how it swept through the field, the long grass that grew on the gentle slopes rising up on either side of the road, beyond the dried-up creek that now, in August, looked like a pebbly foot trail. At night this same wind blew so ferociously against the window panes it made a knocking sound, as if it too was trying to escape.

The field was almost in sight. "I bought a lock for my room," she said.

Da-Nhât stopped walking.

"And now my key is gone."

He looked alarmed. "Do they steal something? Has anyone tried to hurt you?"

"No, no, no. Nothing like that. It's just . . . I mean, I doubt it was Herr Müller. But the key is missing. Maybe it was

Berbyl. Or Joachim, he looks at me sometimes. I can't say. All that I know is that it's gone."

"And you think it was *Herr Müller?*"

"No." She shook her head in frustration, suddenly unsure of what she wanted from Da-Nhât.

"Shall I talk to Berbyl?"

Elke knew Berbyl resented how her father continued to offer Sigrid's dresses to her. But it was more than that. She often wondered if Berbyl blamed her for her mother's absence. The last thing Elke wanted was to make things worse between them. "Forget it. Don't mention it to her. I can always buy another lock."

He gazed at her with a strange expression she couldn't make out. Then, bending toward the ditch, he plucked, strand by strand, a handful of flowering grasses that he brought to his face before giving a sigh. "I, I remember in room of university residence, look at you picture smiling at me, you blonde hairs like snow, so young. In my country they say the moon is full of blond-haired womens and that is why it is so bright."

"I know," she laughed nervously. "You told me at my parents.'"

Afterward, in his hotel room, he had asked about her past boyfriends before encouraging her to pose nude for his camera. She'd knocked over his lamp while getting into position; then her knees wouldn't stop shaking no matter how much she tried to appear poised, the way she imagined Parisian girls would be, posing gracefully in the curtain-filtered light. She'd wanted so much to please him.

She knew her nakedness wasn't wrong because this Elke could only exist here, in this hotel room with this man. This Svengali. Hadn't her mother, buttons done up all the way to her neck, licked his finger? In Da-Nhât's hotel room, she was someone who could live without her mother, free as the sunshine now painting her belly stark white. She *was* a virgin, this Elke never having met the boy she slept with last year whose parents owned the shoe store on Stargarderstrasse. "No," she had told Da-Nhât, believing it truthfully. "You are the first."

If she continued to be this Elke, Da-Nhât's white-haired moon girl, he might take her away, farther away than any German boy she knew would go.

"I think I will know soon, about the job in Hamburg," he said.

"Why not a job in Paris," she said. "You already speak French. Or Canada. A German wife won't help you much in Germany." As soon as she'd said it, she realized she'd been hasty, brought the proposal out into the open too soon, like camera film suddenly exposed to light.

He just smiled and started humming, walking ahead of her.

When they got to the pasture, they found the gate ajar and all the cows were loose. Together they ran after them, switching the cows with willow branches, while the animals ran every which way, their full udders bouncing and their teats spraying milk. Twenty minutes later, they got the herd headed in the right direction.

"You have milk on your face," he said.

"So do you."

They laughed and she wiped his cheek with the sleeve of her sweater.

They were still laughing when they saw Herr Müller in the yard.

"Come, let's put the cows where they belong," Herr Müller said, his shoulders slumped, when they had crossed the yard. "Then I'll show you the milking machines."

Herr Müller toured Da-Nhât around the barn, pointing out this tube, this vacuum, that teat cup. Then he took Da-Nhât by the elbow and led him to one of the stalls. Elke trailed after the two men with her hat and her willow switch still in her hands. She bit her upper lip as she watched the manure stain Da-Nhât's shoes – Oxfords she was sure were worth more money than her mother earned in a month of cleaning houses.

The shaggy brown Holstein bellowed in her stall; Herr Müller rested his arm on her back. "Elke," he called. "Please tell Joachim to come."

She nodded. The day was hot, cicadas buzzing in the poplar trees. She looked across the yard, past threshing machines and bales of hay. Joachim wasn't in the yard but on top of the barn, his legs dangling over the edge of the low-sloping roof.

"Come down," she yelled. "Your father wants you."

He spit.

She stuck out her tongue and regretted it instantly, realizing her action was unbefitting a professional.

Joachim grinned. He stood up and slowly swayed his hips, left, right, left. She held both hands up to her eyes, squinting at his dance. Then he pulled out her key from his overall pocket and dangled it in the air, her secret flashing in his hand, before putting it back in his pocket again.

Joachim! She clenched her hands around her apron and opened her mouth to yell, furious that Joachim had caught her out, but Herr Müller would hear, and how would she explain the lock? She swallowed her anger instead.

"Come up," he said.

She shook her head.

"If you don't come up, I keep the key."

"Are you sure?" she said. "I have a boyfriend who knows judo."

Joachim mimed a martial artist.

From across the yard, she heard the Holstein moan. "Just come, you silly boy."

After he came down the ladder, he took off his shirt and stood bare-chested in his overalls. She could have inscribed her name in the dirt on his shoulders.

"Why do you lock yourself in?" he asked.

She crossed her arms over her chest. "Your father wants you."

Joachim held his arms out like Frankenstein's monster. "Are you scared of me?"

She opened her hand, her palm stretched out toward him. "Give me my key."

"No," he said. "I want to know about the lock." A breeze blew between them, in the space between the barn and the house. A bird twittered and pecked at some fallen grain.

"Are you really going to New York with him?" He rolled a stalk of grass in his mouth. "I'd like to see Yankee Stadium one day."

"But your mother will be lucky to have you here, to help her when she comes home."

"My mother's strong." He looked in the direction of the barn. "It's my father who hides his troubles."

She rested her hand on Joachim's forearm. "If there's anything I can do."

He pulled his arm away. "You want the key?" he said, suddenly a teenager again. "Take it." The key lay in the middle of his dirt-creased palm. As she reached for the key he snatched his hand back and then hurried toward the barn. She followed, surprised and confused at his reaction.

In the coolness of the barn, the smell of hay was sweet. Straw caught in her socks and scratched the exposed skin of her legs. Suddenly the willow switch still twisted around her wrist made her feel awkward, so she unravelled it and set it down on the straw by the door. She offered the Holstein her hand. The cow licked it like a dog. When she pulled her hand away it was green, and, in disgust, she rubbed her palm against her skirt.

Da-Nhât watched intently over Herr Müller's shoulder as he readied the vial of bull sperm. Then Herr Müller rolled up his sleeves and jammed his arm elbow deep into the cow's vagina. The cow bellowed. Joachim helped his father steady the cow. Herr Müller pushed and prodded. Elke stood very still.

"To make her pregnant," he said, shrugging a little with his words.

Da-Nhât smiled. He set his backpack down on the straw between his feet, opened the buckles, and withdrew a camera. He began to adjust the focus and then stopped. He hung the camera around his neck and bent down to look for something else in his pack.

"Could . . . you wait a moment?" he asked Herr Müller.

He withdrew a French-German dictionary, an argyle sweater, a fountain pen, a hard-boiled egg, and a leather journal, placing each item on the ground next to him, near the cow's hind leg. While everyone looked on curiously, Da-Nhât stood up and checked his pockets.

His brow furrowed as he bent down once more. "Sorry. One moment." Joachim and his father shared a puzzled look.

When Da-Nhât found what he had been searching for, he replaced the sweater, the egg, and all the other items in his pack. Then he mounted the flash bulb to the top of his camera. "You may begin."

As the sun was setting, Herr Müller enlisted Da-Nhât's help in loading the truck with potatoes, though Da-Nhât was a slight man who barely weighed more than the sacks themselves. He raised twelve into the truck, impressing Herr Müller, who wiped his hands on his trousers and told Da-Nhât that if he wanted to stay, he'd give him a job.

When Müller drove away, Da-Nhât circled around the tire tracks in the dust to where Joachim stood. "You have something of Elke's?" Da-Nhât said, holding his hand open.

Joachim smiled, stepped back two paces, and flashed the key from his overall pocket before closing his fist around it.

Joachim ran. Da-Nhât followed.

They ran toward the pasture until all she could see were two shapes tussling in the grass. She wondered whether the crib would remain empty, whether Sigrid would drag it back to its proper place near the bed. She wondered if she would marry Da-Nhât. If she could be happy apart from her mother,

her family, her country. Who would she be in America? And what kind of a man would Da-Nhât become if they stayed? What would she regret?

But watching the boys on the bright green field, it was easy to push aside her worries, and think of nothing but fall's approach carried on the blossom-scented air, and the creamy skin of her own white hand covering her mouth.

THE PEACH TREES OF NHAT TAN

I know the Mekong River, how it flows full to overflowing during the rainy season, the poor clinging to her banks near our city of Saigon.

I know how to make a poultice from the powdered marrow of tiger bones or the roughest part of a bear paw, how to pound it smooth until the sinews are supple.

I know how to prepare a balm to soothe all burns, with a scent that tingles the nose the way the air does after an ambush of rain.

I am a healer.

Today, I eat crocodile with a new set of carved ivory chopsticks. But there was a time before. Before my family regained its fortune; days with no money and few ways to earn it, when my family was hungry and hardly better off than those who died in the famine of 1945. When my eldest son drove a *cyclo* through the streets, my second son sold peanuts at the train station, and my youngest son worked the tourists arriving from Hanoi; sometimes old men bought him a soda for his troubles. My father-in-law earned coins by weighing people with a bathroom scale in the flower market on Hang Luoc Street, in the ancient quarter of Saigon. My mother-in-law and I sold traditional medicine from a cart, while I carried my daughter on my back.

There are countless ways of saying the word *mistress*. But I can't let myself feel hate for her, even when I want to, because hate is too simple. Even in the throes of love, I could never allow myself any purity of feeling; this was my failure.

The women at the market told me things I didn't want to know. So did the other gossipers — hairdressers, waitresses, and *cyclo* drivers. Saigon, for all of its people, is not so large that it can hide someone like my husband's mistress. You can't help but talk about someone like her.

My husband's mistress. They smile at her at the Saigon River, where women bathe their children and scrub clothes on stones. They smile at her in the market, where, with manicured fingers, she flicks at melons to measure their sweetness.

She moves like no other creature. There are other women who train their eyes to the sky and let their breasts lead their footsteps, and certainly other women sway as she does when they walk, with their backs curved in the shape of a bow. But it's not just how she holds herself that makes her stand out. Nor is it the way she seems to float above the street — half-flight, half-dance — as if wind moves beneath the soles of her feet, carrying her over the ground like a fluttering peach blossom.

She loves like a mouth, luring people in with gossip that makes them laugh so their bellies move. Perhaps she didn't try to cause trouble – that is what I tell myself – but still, her words glinted as they wandered through the crowds, dangerous as a snake, her stories biting those who could not bite back.

I used to study the charcoal sketches my husband drew of her body, and though I have never seen her naked, I know her breasts are as pendulous as yellow pears, and what lies between her legs as lush as a mulberry grove. At the time I thought, *She has everything a woman could want. She is everything a woman should be.* I told myself, *She is not unlovable, like me.*

I was barely more than a schoolgirl when we married. Perhaps that was why I lost myself in my husband's embrace with such ferocious speed, falling into him as if into a clear, deep pool.

My husband – whose laugh I admired, in whose intellect I stood in awe, who commanded love and loyalty from all who knew him. The day my father introduced me to him and told me we were to be married, he pierced my heart with an intensity I thought – I dared think – I could claim.

He possessed me with ease, and even after I learned of his mistress I continued to throw myself at him, like beads from a broken necklace.

Before my children were born, I had been a healer, collecting medicinal herbs from the garden, using recipes my family has passed down through generations to prepare ointments and balms that I stored in ancient, hand-blown bottles from before the arrival of the French, stamped with Chinese characters. Those I labelled "morning glory" contained my special seeds collected from the vines that grew outside our window, good for calming the nerves, providing a restful sleep, or if taken in large enough doses, for letting you forget your worries and sadness. I tended the vines closely, and when it was time for the blooms to fade and the seed pods to form, I would place a bed sheet underneath them and, carefully snipping the tip of the pod open with scissors, shake the seeds loose. My method of waiting until the pods had almost cracked open before letting the seeds spill free distinguished my harvesting from other healers. It was the one virtue I had, this gift of patience, of waiting, of allowing the longed-for thing to grow stronger.

I can still picture how the rays of the setting sun glinted off my husband's face on the day, for love of him, I turned my back on the knowledge my family had passed down to me. How his features sharpened, his eyes narrowed against the glare as he came to stand next to me, next to the morning glory. My hands trembled with nervousness as I shook the pods, the black seeds spilling wantonly onto the white sheet, like lovers falling onto a bed. My husband thought my practice of making traditional medicine vulgar and primitive, and I wished I could open his eyes to the value of my skills.

Proud of my ancestral knowledge, I glanced up from the seeds I'd gathered in my arms and asked my husband if he liked the colour of the blooms, which were red instead of the common blue. "And the shape of their leaves is like a heart too," I said. "Look how high the vines reach."

My husband sneered at the heart-shaped leaves and the dried-out pods; then without meeting my gaze he said, "Your hands look like they belong to a farmer. Keep wasting your time in the garden and those are the only seeds you'll bear."

After that day, I let the knowledge I'd inherited from my grandfather moulder, and when the seeds inside my old medicine bottles dried to dust I poured many of them out, emptying the seeds down the drain, myself with them. What I couldn't bear to discard, I hid away in a closet. But even without my care, the vines under our bedroom window—fed by the soil and the sun—continued to flourish. And flourishing, they behaved like women in love, bending their foolish heads low, as if gossiping. But they also appeared sad, the oppressive heat forcing their already supplicant heads to bow until they nearly touched the ground.

Our home lies off a wide, tree-lined boulevard, from which only a small corner of its red tile roof can be seen. Two marble lions flank the entrance, guarding us from evil spirits, and peanut vines line the path that leads to our wood-shuttered front door.

Here, in this house, is where I slept with my four children and my husband's parents after he left. Here is where my garden ends and the rest of the world begins, at the threshold of our crumbling villa built by the French a century ago, which hides behind manioc bushes and a fence of live bamboo. I let dust mar the petals of the hibiscus, while the flowers died under flocks of hoopoes and jacanas. Behind palms corseted with growth rings, the children played under sunlight that punched down like a fist. Dancing heat waves rose from the dusty path, and in the corner of the garden, in the cooler spaces, indigo shadows sheltered my grief.

My husband's mistress modeled for him in this house. Naked, she would pose for him in the garden, her arm slung over the back of the chair, in full view of the kitchen, where I would pretend not to see them. While they took no notice of me, I would secretly watch his hand sketch her in charcoal and touch her lines with his fingers, stroke after black stroke.

Once, I had been his model.

When I asked my husband why he needed a new model, he said, "Sen has the kind of body that catches the light." He drew slowly from his cigarette and then pulled his hand away from his lips, gazing at the ember as it glowed. "Naturally, a model must be comfortable with her body," my husband continued, resting his hand on the back of the chair where she would soon sit. "But it's more than mere comfort with the body. She has the capacity for stillness."

His words left me hollow. I felt ashamed, angry at myself for not being more than I was. What more could I give? I wanted to reach out and hold his hand, but I could tell by the way his eyes flicked away from me that I disgusted him.

Later, I lingered in the garden, refusing to give them their privacy. I stood at the cistern, scrubbing the scales off a fish we would eat for dinner, cursing the knife in my hand while the two of them sat by the pond. She was half-naked, a black silk tunic slipping from her shoulders to reveal pale skin made paler by the dark fabric.

Suddenly the peonies, the jackfruit trees, the lush beauty of the garden I had always loved became ugly.

I turned away. If there had been a room I could have fled to, a private space that would have sheltered me, I would have run there and cried. But the sorrow in my veins would have followed me, as would the image of my husband leaning intimately toward Sen as if I wasn't there. "An artist is, above all things, entitled to the right to be free," he said, grinning. I knew then he would refuse himself nothing, least of all for any thought of me.

Over the next few months, I would secretly take sketches out of his portfolio when my husband was at work. In this way, I followed the progress of their relationship. I made myself stare at the proof of his infidelities, as if by doing so I could eventually lessen the force with which his betrayal struck me each time. Drawings of Sen on the ground, fondling herself, her back arched, her face contorted by imminent ecstasy. My husband's own image in the picture, a self-portrait, looming over her – and though his face was not visible, victory was written into the size of his body, the inflated space he claimed at the centre of his artwork.

Each time I put the portfolio away, I steadied myself by touching the temple pots that stood next to the altar table, as if the cool porcelain in the family shrine could drain the heat of my anger from my palms. Then I knelt and prayed to my ancestors for strength and wisdom; still, my husband grew more and more unhappy. He lifted his chopsticks as though they were leaden weights. He would slump his head when he sat at the piano to play his favourite song, "Go Schooling in the East" — as if playing a patriotic song of resistance instead of a love song could hide what he felt in his heart.

It wasn't until much later that I would understand it was the burden of my devotion, the crushing weight of my over-whelming love for him that had pushed the two of them together. With his mistress there was no shame: she did not need him. And in not being needed, in simply being played with, he was made eager and free.

One night as I was preparing dinner, I saw my husband oiling his hair in the front hall mirror. Our lives could not continue like this: my own children had begun to eye the ghost I was becoming with suspicion and fear. So I offered my husband his freedom as a final test, to give him the chance to show me that he cared. For him, I would slip a noose slowly around my own neck and give him the chance to save me. "Go to her. Be with her, now." But instead of giving me respect, instead of acknowledging what I had said, he continued to tuck a lock of stray hair back in its place, as if I were a mere irritation just as easily dismissed.

Then he smiled at me, meeting my gaze without a hint of shame.

Unable to control myself, I grabbed a knife from the coun-ter and lunged at him. In his eyes I saw fear racing toward me, the very violence of my love for him. For an instant I was beyond threats, angry enough to kill. But he caught hold of my wrist and the moment passed; the passion trembled through his body and mine, and then it was gone. He looked from the point of the knife to me, and his expression told me he knew I would not hurt him. He was safe, and finally free.

I stepped back and turned the knife on myself, holding it to my wrist. He did not try to lower the blade or take it away from me. He simply turned his back and walked out the door. I let the knife fall to the ground, ashamed I had drawn no blood with the blade.

After he left, after the children had gone to bed, the house was solid with silence. I tried to sleep, my head aching with the knowledge that I filled my husband not even with a sense of duty, that he saw my sharp knees and elbows as a cage, jutting reminders of his obligation to me. I would never be what he lusted after. The pillows of her flesh made him restless while my body simply bored him.

He did not come home that evening. Wanting to numb my pain, I retrieved the one bottle of morning glory seeds I had kept in my closet and dissolved the ground seeds into a glass of cold water. The seeds were so old they had little taste. But they were still powerful.

That night, my mind empty, I watched the colours on the ceiling change from blue to red, mistaking every sound I heard in the house for my husband having come home.

As the weeks passed, my four children watched me read sutras, chant scriptures, and grow gaunt with waiting. To honour his memory, I forced myself to rise out of bed and wash my face each morning, remembered to eat even though the rice lodged in my throat like fish bones. At night, I would pretend my husband still lay next to me, and sometimes I could almost imagine his breathing. But then I would open my eyes wide to find myself staring only at blackness, and once again alone.

How long would I have to wait until he returned? The sun
set. Another day gone.

I drew hope like water from a well. The nights were the
worst. When I closed my eyes, scenes of the two of them
making love played like a film in my mind. I would see how
he caressed her, the way she responded – the girlish laugh,
the uncontrollable shortness of breath. Their bodies
twined, coiled and glistening like salamanders.

Days turned into weeks, and then into months.

My family and I had no means by which to survive. In the
months after he left, we bartered our tables, chairs, and
beds for food. We sold the ceremonial temple pots, the lions
that guarded our home, and the ivory chopsticks my great-
grandparents had fed each other with at their wedding.
Hunger burned our stomachs. We ate the racing pigeons
from my husband's fly pen and moved through the empty
house like echoes.

My sons and father-in-law went out into the city to earn
money however they could. Still, we ate poor man's fare:
cabbage, sesame salt, dried shrimp, or plain boiled rice and
duckweed that I purposefully prepared with too much salt so
we would spoon less into our bowls. The roof tiles cracked
and the rain leaked in. Yet my eldest son defended his father
and wouldn't let me speak ill of him, not even to wonder
when he would come home. My son would point his chopsticks at me accusingly and say, "It's not your place to speak
of these things. What does a woman know?" At times, I
thought he might hit me. Instead, he burned off his resent-
ment driving his *cyclo* through the dirty streets of Saigon,

feeling the wind blowing dust into his face, until the pain in his back nailed him to his bed.

Shortly after, I began to sell wares at the market on Nguyen Hue Street. I cut my hair so that it would swing over my jaw, disguising my features. Over my newly shorn hair, I pulled a broad-brimmed hat down as low as it would go over my face. I tried to sell orchids from the garden, but after days of counting a handful of coins from an almost-empty purse, I knew I had to sell my family's traditional medicines.

Most of the cures I sold had been prepared by my grandfather, though I had neglected both his ointments and my own, allowing them to moulder in their jars, breeding fungi like exotic mushrooms in a garden. But I sold what I had from my cart, these remedies from my family's secret recipes, my mother-in-law helping when she could, while I carried my already-toddling daughter on my back.

At the market we were surrounded by cloth weavers, trash sweepers, and vendors of manioc, yam, and maize. The other sellers looked our way in curiosity, but I ignored them. I wanted no one to recognize me, to know I was my husband's wife.

Across the road from us was an old woman who sold shrimp croquettes and spring rolls with her seven-year-old granddaughter, who always wore chopsticks in her hair. "Did you sleep well?" the woman called to her neighbour while she heated up a vat of oil.

"Four hours," said the man who polished shoes. "But I'm as spry as a cock." He flexed nonexistent muscles and chuckled. When he had finished setting up his stand, he sat down on the curb to eat his breakfast, a bowl of thin rice gruel. He saw me watching him and waved. "You there – and how are you this morning?"

I nodded and quickly turned away, disgusted by the way his soup dribbled over his gums and down his chin. He had no teeth.

For days I kept to myself.

Then one afternoon, I fell asleep. When I awoke, I was startled to find someone standing beside my cart.

"I was keeping an eye on your cart while you rested."

"You're the man who writes letters," I said, squinting at his silhouette against the sun. He was charming, boyish almost, with a slim body and smooth chest, skin the colour of rice paper, and a bouncing step – it was hard to remain unfriendly. Soon I realized that every vendor working on Nguyen Hue Street had their own story of struggle to tell, and their quiet courage only highlighted my own self-pity and made me lower my gaze in shame. Looking at my feet, I remembered Lao Tse's words, how even the longest journey must begin where you stand.

Tet had come. Everyone was anxious to get a haircut or buy new clothes to mark the Vietnamese New Year. During the week of Tet, the crowds of shoppers at the market became thicker and more frantic with each passing night, holding up traffic as they jostled each other to find the items they still needed. Vendors worked themselves to exhaustion; from across the road, I'd watch as the girl with the chopsticks in her hair would let her head fall to her chest before she caught herself, though her grandmother was always too busy deep-frying spring rolls to notice. Around us, fishmongers carried baskets on either end of the poles balanced across their shoulders, shouting, "Fish for sale." Festive red banners celebrating the New Year sprang up on stalls, where people bought candied fruits, cone-shaped kumquats, and of course peach trees, the symbol of life and good fortune.

Vendors from the north flooded the market, with peach trees roped to their bicycle panniers, transforming the street into a river of blossoms. It reminded me of other Tet celebrations, and of how my husband and I used to pick a peach tree together and display it proudly in our home, our guests complimenting us on how well we had chosen.

The merchant beside my cart told me his peach trees had been grown in the soils of Nhat Tan. In Nhat Tan, he explained, they say only happy villagers are permitted to cultivate the peach trees that will be sold at Tet and praised by the gods, for the heavens cannot bless trees grown by quarrelling wives and husbands who have abandoned love.

"There are three species," he said. "The red, the pink, and the white. The red tree forms a round canopy, its flowers thick with petals. The pink is better known for its fruit. Of the three species, it is the white-flowered tree that grows with the most difficulty." He told me the most delicate task is making the blooms appear ten days before Tet. For this, the horticulturist must make an incision around the tree's trunk and then strip off all the leaves. He must be careful, though, because a cut too deep will injure the tree, while a cut too shallow will be ineffective. "But even skill cannot graft a budding branch to the tree if both cannot be kept alive long enough for the grafting to take."

I was about to thank the man for sharing his wisdom when the girl with the chopsticks in her hair suddenly fainted. There was nothing I could do except watch her hands shoot out like freed birds when her face fell into the vat of hot oil.

Her grandmother pulled her out of the oil and laid her on the street. Immediately the child recoiled into a fetal position – screaming, screaming – her face covered in hot fat that streamed down her neck and shoulders and chest, leaving red trails on her skin, her black hair dripping with burning oil.

I took one of my grandfather's jars and ran to the girl. Kneeling beside her, I untwisted the lid and then stroked back her hair. The burn was so fresh, her skin still smelled sweet. Her face had not yet blistered.

I ladled the topmost layer of fungus from the jar and spread the fermented balm over the girl's face, wondering what my hands were doing and whether it mattered. Then I remembered what my grandfather had often said, reciting the words of Buddha: "Knowledge is power."

The girl cried and whimpered, and by degrees grew still. Her grandmother wept.

The next day when the girl awoke, her skin was unblemished, smooth as the day she was born.

When my husband heard that I was now able to fill my porcelain bowls with not only rice but silver coins, he crawled back like an insect. He took off his shoes, wet from the rain, and stood in front of me as if he'd never left at all.

Fighting aroused his lust. He took me in his arms and though I pretended he disgusted me, I let him touch my flesh. The moment he entered me I knew I was powerful, that he could not stop now, would not pull away from me even if his life depended on it. He opened his eyes and they flashed in rage at me, the woman who no longer had any need of him.

I did not come. This was how I stayed strong and did not collapse with longing. An instinct not to be broken.

In the morning he once again sat with the family at the breakfast table. My mother- and father-in-law ate betel nuts and nodded in passive approval, or was it resignation I saw on their faces? Such friends of suffering.

Later, when we were alone, he asked for our money. I watched the shape of his mouth betray his shame, the guilt of his abandonment of us written into the thinning curve of his lips. Had he kissed his mistress with those lips and promised to return, even as he discarded her as casually as an umbrella once the sun has begun to shine?

"I am the rightful and continuing head of this family," he said.

But I know the Mekong River. I know how to make a poultice from the powdered marrow of tiger bones or the roughest part of a bear paw, how to pound it smooth until the sinews are supple. I was the one who rubbed salve into the little girl's burned skin and whispered, "Your face will be beautiful again, someday." I know how the grafted branch of a peach tree tips its soul into the cut made by the gardener's knife and spills itself into the wound, driven by the simple yearning to become part of a greater life.

HIS LOVER'S GHOST

L ucille always has an excuse for why she can't visit
Raymond, in spite of the fact that her son is dying. Vince
and Raymond have had polite, frosty visits at her house, for
Thanksgiving, Christmas, maybe twice or three times a
year, but this is the first time she's come to them, and only
because Vince called her every day. He's sure she invents
obligations for herself. Her two Persian cats, for instance:
high-maintenance animals that can't be left on their own,
and now the kitten, which is still not housebroken and
needs a special lotion applied to its eyes on the hour.

"And I'm working on a new project," she says. She's been
devouring popular fiction set in the Ming dynasty, calling
it research. For what kind of a project, she doesn't say.

Raymond shifts on his bed, which they've pulled into the
living room for her visit, and she watches him uncomfortably

as he strains to grasp his leather portfolio on the end table. "I've started a project of my own," Raymond tells Lucille. "It's a family tree. It's just . . . I wish I had more information."

She takes the pile of loose leaf from his hands. Photographs culled from shoeboxes are carefully glued to the top of each sheet of paper, and underneath each picture he's hand-written a few notes in ball point pen: Born 1932. Collected matchbooks. Played the tuba. Liked oranges.

Vince bought him the portfolio to encourage this activity, hoping Lucille might want to help with the project.

"Francie didn't marry in '49. It was '48."

Raymond props himself up on his elbow. "That's what I mean. What I was thinking was, maybe we could look at the pages together?"

"Mmm-hmmm. Mmm-hmmm." Lucille nods her head, shuffling the papers. Her too-heavy eyeliner overdraws the Asian slant. Her nimble fingers, her slight build, her quick jittery movements remind Vince of a little black mouse, though in the sun her dyed-black hair looks more purple than black, the colour of crushed berries.

"You could help me with the facts," Raymond says.

"Sure, sure," she says, shutting him down. "But you know. I don't know much more than you."

Such a response is just what Vince expected.

She put the papers down on the glass coffee table, Windex streaks still visible on its surface. Her eyes scrutinize their home: the brick walls, the exposed ductwork, the wine racks overhanging the kitchen island, the pulley system on the ceiling by the front door where they store their two mountain bikes, unused since Raymond's diagnosis. Their studio used to be a glass factory during Gastown's boom years a century ago.

No words remain to fill the awkward silence that follows. Lucille has already told Raymond about her upcoming trip to Kenya. She has taken one trip a year, dutifully, since her husband died. "Ngorongoro Crater," she announced, mispronouncing the location. "This October. All the animals will be there."

The silence crackles between them.

To give himself a break from the tension, Vince stands up. "I'll go make us a snack."

"I'm not hungry, are you hungry?" Raymond says.

"Don't trouble yourself, I can't really stay," Lucille says. "Like I said, you can't leave the kitten on her own for too long."

In the safety of the kitchen, a semi-partitioned area in the corner of the loft, Vince prepares a fruit-and-cheese plate to go with their cappuccinos. He can waste ten, even fifteen minutes this way, if he cuts the pieces small. But then he hears Raymond break his promise by telling Lucille about the ghost.

"Raymond," Vince calls from the kitchen, "you want strawberries or cantaloupe?"

But Raymond persists. "At first he was only a black smudge on a chair."

"Honey, did you say strawberries? Do you want them sliced, with sugar on the side?"

"Yesterday, Mom, he whispered in my ear."

"Sliced or whole? What was that?"

Three months ago the ghost made its first appearance, and the sicker Raymond gets, the more often it comes. The books that Vince has started to read behind Raymond's back say that the dying are often visited by the dead, as if the dead are welcoming them, but Raymond is anything but comforted by the presence of the ghost. Vince takes this as a good sign. He already feels like he's losing Raymond, piece by piece.

These days, when Vince looks at his lover, he sees both inside and outside Raymond's body at once. Vince watches the shoulder-heaving struggle of each small breath, and in his mind's eye he sees past Raymond's chest to the distended vena cavae and pulmonary veins, beyond the breastbone to three-inch strips of white connective tissue covered in nodules, waterlogged. He sees Raymond's deoxygenated blood running rampant with bacteria, his ventricles rebelling against the declining authority of his sinoatrial node. It's a *coup d'état* of the body.

He hasn't told Raymond that he's haunted by the waking nightmare of seeing his lifeless body on an ambulance gurney. It's a vision that paralyzes Vince no matter what he's doing – washing his lover, standing in line at the grocery store, spooning food into Raymond's mouth – and forces him to clutch the sink or reach out for a chair to balance himself before the room starts to spin. But he's never told Raymond, because the mind can play tricks; can make you believe things are worse than they are, can make you give up hope before all hope is truly lost. Take Y2K, though the millennium is still more than a year away, the world is already screaming about the end times. He reminds himself to ask the doctor again about Raymond's medication – maybe it's a dosage problem that's causing him to imagine the ghost. Or it could be a viral hallucination – the ghost often rides in on Raymond's fevers.

By the time Vince returns with cantaloupe squares and grapes, strawberries halved and fanned out on a glass plate, Raymond has told his mother what he's already told Vince: he thinks he's seen the ghost at least once before. He remembers his dad getting a phone call at home, how he'd piled Raymond and his sisters into the red station wagon and driven them to the Hotel Europe on skid row, not far from where they are living now. Raymond strains to say so much.

"Honey," Vince says. "Your mom doesn't want to hear about all that."

"A man was dragged out of the tenement house in hand-cuffs," Raymond continues. "Covered in his own crap."

Lucille twists the wedding band that she still wears round and round on her finger. Vince worries that if Lucille thinks Raymond's going crazy too, she will be even more reluctant to visit than she is now. "Your father had a brother," she finally answers, her voice strained. "Once or twice he came to the house but your father sent him away. They didn't get along. Your father thought he'd be a bad influence on you kids. Your uncle was a bad seed from the very beginning. Your father didn't like to speak about him and I didn't pry." She sighs, looking up at the ceiling. "Charlie was sent to Woodlands. But I don't know the details. A lunatic asylum is not the kind of thing you talk about over dinner. Anyway, why would Charlie visit you?"

When Raymond and his mother stare each other down, their eyebrows wrinkle their foreheads with the same tense conviction.

Raymond has told Vince before the Chinese believe that a soul with no tomb to call his own is destined to forever roam the earth. Vince understands this idea of not wanting to let go. He imagines his fingers pried from Raymond's lifeless ankles: he will have to be dragged, clawing and biting, away from his dead lover.

"I don't remember anything else," Lucille says. Her leopard-skin shoes tap nervously on the glazed concrete floor. Then she dismisses Raymond's ghost with a laugh. "I guess if your dad took you with him to the Hotel Europe, I must have been at work. I don't know if he said anything to me. He must have. We always talked about things, we didn't keep secrets." But the way she presses her eyes shut suggests otherwise to Vince.

Over the years Vince has heard enough of Raymond's stories. As a family, they didn't speak what was on their minds, they shouted it, drowning out their true meaning. His father never accepted Raymond's sexuality. And after he broke up with Libby, the dental hygienist, and moved out of the apartment they had shared, quit college, and started performing in drag, his father had disowned him. And Lucille, being a traditional wife, never spoke out against her husband. Never pleaded with him, not even in whispered words, not even on his death bed, to reconcile with his son. "I wish she'd tried," Raymond once confided to Vince, "you know, to help my dad come around, so we could make our peace."

She scratches her head and Vince sees black dye collect under her fingernails. "I wish I could remember more, but I don't. I'm losing everything these days, not just my memory," she says, changing the subject. "My memory, my car keys, even my temper. It never ends. I never lost my temper at all when your father was alive."

The urge to say, "Maybe you should have, just once, for

Raymond's sake," burns on Vince's tongue. But he bites down hard and winces, keeps his thoughts to himself.

Nestor, the homecare worker, arrives at 7:50 a.m., punctual as always, knocking out a familiar rhythm on the door: *Shave-and-a-haircut-ten-cents.* His cheeks are red as he comes inside, saying, "Hallo, hallo, hallo," and puts four bags of groceries on the counter, shopping being just one of the many things Nestor Matapang does for Raymond and Vince. Raymond, half-asleep on the couch since seven, pulls himself together, wipes his mouth with his hand, runs his fingers through his hair.

"You looking good today," Nestor says.

"Well, I try."

"I have a thing for you that is exciting." Nestor flamboyantly whips a CD out of his pocket.

"You found it!" Raymond beams.

"Kenny Rogers? Since when do you like country music?" How can you live with someone for twenty years and still be surprised by them?

"It's an album I used to listen to when I was a teenager," Raymond says apologetically.

"I didn't find it at home," Nestor says triumphantly. "Even after I look. So I go out and buy you one."

Vince isn't sure if he likes Nestor. He is probably a nice, decent person, but Vince considers everything he has to do for Raymond—from tacking down the scatter rugs, removing electrical cords from under foot, and scouring the grocery shelves for non-slippery wax, to massaging out the cramps from his toes and wiping the sweat from his brow while he sleeps – as his responsibility and his privilege. He acquiesces to Nestor's visits only because he can't do it alone.

Nestor Matapang likes ping pong and euchre and watching golf on TV. He holds a bachelor's degree from a university in the Philippines, where he worked as a lab technician, but he says he cares for his patients intuitively, with the healing power of God. And to Vince's dismay, he listens to Raymond's ghost stories. At first, Vince worried that Nestor might have Raymond sent to long-term care if he thought Raymond was losing his hold on reality. But Nestor had worked at Woodlands Hospital for eight years as a psych assistant before the institution closed for good. His ideas about what was normal were more liberal than most people's. Nestor wasn't bothered by Raymond's questions and even seemed flattered by all the interest. "What did the patients eat? What kind of treatment did they get? Did anyone ever escape?" Charlie's ghost and the curiosity he engendered brought Raymond and Nestor closer together, and though Raymond was still frightened of the ghost whenever he made an appearance, he was no longer as scared of Charlie as he had been. And the more at peace he became with the ghost, the more insecure Vince felt.

Raymond hung on Nestor's every word, and at the end of the day, he was bursting with news. "Patients had their teeth pulled so they couldn't bite staff," he told Vince. "They had *experiments* conducted on them. Ones you wouldn't perform on a dog. They once locked up a woman for giving birth out of wedlock."

Vince hated it. The morbidity. How easily Nestor could steal what was left of Raymond's attention. After all, this was

Vince's final audience with Raymond, too. No one, no matter what they say, really died alone. Raymond, daily, took little pieces of Vince with him.

"Today, I make you Filipino rice," Nestor says as Raymond watches him unpack the groceries with an intimacy that makes Vince uncomfortable, like a lover, still enraptured by the other's newness; watching the fingers around a green pepper, the curved lips while humming a tune. Maybe it's how Raymond looked at him years ago.

Vince gathers his briefcase and puts on his overcoat. The migraine that attacked last night is asserting itself forcefully over his left eye. Maybe it's just the stress: the lack of sleep; the soreness in his back from lifting Raymond into the bath creeping into his head; the worry about trying to feed him, when he won't eat; the outrageous cost of drugs and medical home-care supplies. Their life savings are gone. They are living off Vince's credit cards, and Vince has been losing weight steadily for a month. But he will not break his promise to Raymond. As difficult as it sometimes is to witness Raymond's slow decline, he will not give up this heartache for anyone, least of all for Nestor Matapang, Raymond's new flame.

What does Nestor know about how Raymond smells when he sweats at night, the animal odour that fills the room and reeks of something turning, almost spoiled, so unlike the smell Vince has loved and licked from his lover's skin for all these years? Or the panic of waking to the cold, bare pillow next to him at night? No matter that Raymond has just gone to the washroom, Vince is always disoriented, momentarily unsure if the worst has already happened, if Raymond is dead or alive. What does Nestor know about living with the constant threat of losing the person you love most? Who is he to fill Raymond's head with the horrors he saw at Woodlands?

But Nestor is no pushover. Back in the Philippines, he had demonstrated against Marcos, even setting fire to the Malacañang Palace with a large group of other protestors, while wearing a balaclava and throwing Molotov cocktails. Maybe this is why when Vince tells him to stop talking to Raymond about the ghost, Nestor holds Vince's gaze a second too long for his liking and almost mouths the word *but*.

Vince's office is on the second floor of the Germanic studies department and has a view of a parking lot and the roof of the B wing, white with pigeon filth. In the distance he can see a single cherry tree that still has no leaves yet, and a black crow in its bare branches. The smell of freshly brewed coffee gently permeates the hallway outside his office.

"Have you tried Trinity Western in Langley?" says the woman on the other end of the line, the secretary of an evangelical preacher who claims to have seen both Paul the Apostle and God personally. She explains that the preacher is doing revivals in Florida right now, and she tells him she's sorry. He takes note of the name she gives him for future reference, and dials the next number on his list, the home of a fifteen-year-old Ethiopian boy who is said to have cured the musician Slim Sandy of pancreatic cancer. He makes an appointment with the boy's father for three weeks from now.

He calls Lucille and gets her machine. "Lucille, it's Vince calling again. Are you getting these messages? I know you're busy with going to Africa, but, look . . . you can't avoid this situation any longer. It's not going to go away. Christ, it's been two weeks since you've seen him —" The machine cuts him off. Damn.

Last he calls the Santo Daime Church of the Modern Light of the Queen. He looks at his wristwatch. It's time for class, but still he leaves a voice mail, meticulously summarizing the details of Raymond's illness and his hopes for Raymond's full recovery, before descending the stairs to the first floor, where students are already packed tightly together in the hallway, grappling with their books, on their way to the next class.

Usually, he likes to get to class a few minutes early, to settle himself down, remove his overcoat at his leisure and arrange it over the back of his chair. Then he takes his lecture notes from his briefcase and lays them out, in order, on the podium in front of him, writes a few relevant things on the board, things he finds necessary to shift his frame of mind to a teaching one. But today he is late and most of his second-year German language students are already in class, forty-five faces upturned and expectant, pens poised.

Suddenly, he can't remember the lesson plan.

Most weeks he manages to maintain a persona in front of a class, present a façade of professional calm and confidence. To hide his fluster he affects a stern face and shuffles through his papers, begins talking about upcoming assignments. But his fingers are trembling and he drops two pieces of loose leaf to the floor.

Eventually he tells them to open their textbooks and gives them an assignment from the fourth chapter to complete.

The subjunctive mood, he explains, is a feeling used to convey wishful thinking and statements contrary to fact: If I promise ... If I swear ... If only he had twenty more years ...

When he returns to his office, Lucille has left a message with the department secretary. She is volunteering with Kids Up Front this weekend. It's a commitment she just can't get out of, but she'll be in touch soon. At least she called back. He doubts she bothered calling Raymond to tell him herself.

He allows himself a moment to contain his frustration.

With Nestor at the house, he's free to scout back-alley shops for an hour or two after class, and today he has an appointment with a traditional Chinese herbalist.

The shop smells like fungus and has shelves that reach to the ceiling, holding glass jars full of dried starfish flakes and vials of ginseng. A wizened man tells Vince about hu zhang, or "tiger's cane," and Japanese knotweed, which he has for sale as a powder or in capsules. He lowers jars down from the shelf and arranges them for display on the counter.

"Dan shen pien," he says. "This good, too. Have no reaction with other medicine from your doctor."

"They're not treating him," Vince says irritably. "That's the whole point." The team of doctors who had been working to save Raymond's life abandoned him when it became clear he was going to die anyway within the year despite their best efforts. They gave Vince a piece of paper with the address and phone number of a local palliative hospice. After Vince had recovered from the tremendous shock of being told "nothing more could be done," he took Raymond home.

What helped him get through the day was setting little goals and making tentative plans: he will call the next three numbers on his list. Remember to pick up some vitamin D for Raymond, along with some organic soy milk. *After work tonight, we'll eat dinner and I'll get Raymond to eat more than half his meal. We'll watch a TV show that will keep Raymond awake past the first commercial. We'll sit on the couch and plan something for the weekend.*

"We'll visit a costume shop."

"Try on fluorescent plastic boas."

"Go to Playland, ride the wooden roller coaster."

"Eat sushi with our fingers. On a picnic in Stanley Park."

"Are you sure it won't be too cold?" Raymond said.

"Yeah, but we'll have morphine," Vince answered deviously.

It doesn't matter that some of their plans involve things they'll never do. It was the planning that mattered, the fact they were using phrases like "you will" and "we will," and never stopped talking about the future.

Now Vince tries to explain to the man behind the counter, "All we have is morphine. That's it. The doctors aren't giving him anything."

The herbalist catches Vince's gaze and holds it for a long time. His demeanor becomes less businesslike. "I give you some ginseng tea, for yourself," he says. "Ginseng tea and ginseng root will give you strength. It is good for your health, you drink this, please." He weighs a small amount of the waxy-looking root on an old balance scale and puts the chunks he's cut into the size of coins into paper envelopes. Then he places everything into a bag. As he rings up the purchase, the man says, "In our life, four out of five things do not happen as we wish."

Vince gets into his car and hurls the bag with the medicine violently into the back seat. Two of the envelopes tumble onto the floor and under the seat while he is driving. He can already hear Raymond complaining about how he's tired of trying a new alternative treatment every few weeks and visiting every quack in the city. He stops at the store to pick up some candles for Raymond, the stress of the day heavy on his chest like a boulder, and then decides to drive to the liquor store for a bottle of red wine. Why not? He deserves it.

The lights in the liquor store buzz unpleasantly. While he is standing at the till, the room begins to spin and Vince has to clutch the counter to balance himself. He is seized by the vision of Raymond's lifeless body lying on an ambulance gurney, under a wrinkled grey sheet. The body is still warm as it is wheeled out of the apartment by paramedics who, without speaking, walk stiffly into the elevator across the clay tile lobby, out the front door, past the staring people on the sidewalk. A breeze ruffles the sheet and, for a moment, it looks as if Raymond is still alive. Vince cries out and runs after the gurney, but no one hears him. All he can do is watch as Raymond is guided head first into the ambulance and driven away.

It's as if the devil himself is squeezing his throat. He can't breathe.

"You okay?" asks the cashier.

Vince nods and hurries out of the store with his wine, trembling.

When he arrives home he finds Nestor playing his fiddle for Raymond, who is sitting on the couch, grinning but too sick to clap. Country music. God. At least today he didn't come home to find Nestor cutting cantaloupe into animal shapes or drawing happy faces on their tissue boxes. Any childish act Vince finds them engaged in irritates him.

"Come, join us," Nestor says, motioning to Vince, his foot tapping.

"No, I can't," Vince says, closing the door and marching to the dining room table with a stack of papers. For the next two hours, he sits at the table pretending he's marking, trying to hide how isolated he feels.

Later that evening, as they curl up in bed, Vince runs his hand down the length of Raymond's wasted body. His body still craves Raymond, has never stopped. Vince rings Raymond's nipple with his tongue to try to arouse him — this man who at one time had been able to come almost on command — but Raymond breaks out into a cold sweat. The way it dampens the downy line of hair that runs from the top of his chest to below his belly button makes Vince ache in the pit of his stomach. Raymond pants, his breath jagged. Then his slow hands are like spiders on Vince's leg, his lips chapped as they move toward Vince's cock.

"Come here." Vince touches Raymond's face, spotty with exertion. His head is clammy with the effort of it all. "Never mind."

Raymond hasn't been able to maintain an erection in weeks. And now, neither can Vince. They cuddle, but there is something new between them, separating them, as palpable as a stiffly starched bedsheet. After a few minutes Raymond pushes away.

"If you want," Raymond says, staring at the ceiling, "to visit a prostitute, I don't mind."

The clock ticks noisily on the night stand. Out the window, ambulance sirens drone, and then the terrible silence, the heavy darkness of the bedroom engulfs them again.

"Why would you say something like that?" Vince finally says quietly.

"You know why."

"I love *you*."

"And I love you too, that's why."

The words volley back and forth over the net. But then there is no net. Just a wall. And the words hit it and fall.

"Why don't you ever talk to me about Charlie anymore?" Vince says.

"You know you don't like it when I talk about him."

"But I'm here."

"I shouldn't put so much on you."

Vince tears back the covers and gets out of bed. In the bathroom he takes two tranquilizers. In spite of his arsenal of sleep aids, Vince can't sleep. Sometimes he stays up late to research what his eyes can't deny and are forced to acknowledge daily: Raymond's deteriorating vision, his incontinence. He reads medical texts on alternative treatments and outcomes and wakes up feeling terrible the next day.

When he manages to fall asleep on his own, he sometimes finds himself dreaming about them committing suicide together. On a cruise, stepping out over the Pacific, or taking cyanide pills on a beach, a curious seagull the last living thing they see. These dreams of the various ways they could take their own lives are just another reason he forces himself awake.

The moment of sleep, the tipping point between consciousness and oblivion scares him: a siphoning of self.

Every night he feels that he's about to lose something vital and urgent, and he can't let go. Still, he wishes he could rest, find some peace.

"Don't worry," Raymond says, cradling Vince in his arms and stroking his hair. "Sleep now, sleep now," he begins to croon. "It's going to be okay."

Vince wants to say, "You don't have to be a hero." But he doesn't, because he understands without understanding that this rebellion is all Raymond has left.

The next day, while Nestor rushes to and fro, Raymond strains for breath as he pulls his oxygen tank trolley toward the kitchen. Would Vince like a cup of tea?

"Let me do it," Vince says.

"No," Raymond says.

"Sit down," Nestor says, but his tone is not unkind.

Vince leads Raymond back to the couch and strokes his arm, hurt that this caress is all he the comfort Raymond will allow him to give in front of Nestor.

"Stop clucking," Raymond wheezes, "and fussing."

"You stop," Vince says. "Stop showing off." Then he adds quietly, "It's okay, Raymond. You can drop the bravery tactics. You're among friends."

Vince hates how Raymond insists he's strong enough to walk on his own though his breath is laboured, his skin steeped in a patchy rash. The way he sometimes trembles with the sheer effort of pretending his illness isn't as painful as it is. The way he fights to remain who he used to be. Vince wants to console him but can't, because Raymond won't acknowledge his despair.

His efforts to maintain an outward façade of strength are as much a show as his old drag performances at the Boom-Boom Room on Davie Street. Raymond was perform-ing as Connie Chiwa, in nothing but satin shorts, pasties, and a blond wig, swaying his hips to "Where the Boys Are," when Vince walked in, twenty years ago now, and fell in love with his narrow thighs and bitchy banter. It wasn't true that Vince resented all of Raymond's performances, begrudged him his time in the spotlight, his flamboyance, his relish for life. It wasn't jealousy – after all, after eight months of dating, hadn't Raymond begun performing as "Miss Taken"?

Finally, now, it seems as though Raymond has found a new role to play – the martyr, the saint.

"Now, get up," Nestor says, flashing his big white smile. He helps Raymond onto the bed, but only as much as he needs to, allowing Raymond to hold on to what's left of his dignity and strength.

Today Nestor has come to install a syringe driver in Raymond's arm. Vince had been feeding morphine to Raymond in an eyedropper, and Raymond chasing the bitter liquid with lemonade. But since Raymond's nausea has gotten worse, he can no longer keep the oral dose down. So Raymond will now receive a round-the-clock morphine drip through a small pump that only Nestor can set up. The battery-operated unit is covered with buttons, and beeping and flashing lights.

Nestor turns a vial upside down and draws a day's worth of morphine into the syringe. He fiddles with the buttons to provide the correct time-release dosage, then attaches the syringe to the long worm of plastic tubing connected to the machine. "Every day I will come and put more medicine in it," he says. He secures the syringe with a rubber strap to the top of the pump.

"What if it stops beeping?" Vince says.

"No problem, no problem. You just call me."

Nestor takes the other end of the tube and, with a needle, inserts it into Raymond's arm, leaving the hollow plastic tube under the skin. As the syringe pumps morphine into Raymond, Vince watches as his facial muscles relax and his eyes become too heavy to keep open.

"You can carry the pump in a small bag," Nestor continues. "Attach it to this belt, when he wants to move around." He finishes by putting some gauze over the tubing in Raymond's arm, taping it securely, and rolling Raymond's pyjama sleeve back down.

After Nestor leaves, Raymond sleeps and Vince tidies the place, putting the furniture back, the bed in the corner where it belongs. When he moves the nightstand, he drops a framed photo of the two of them in Sutton Hoo, but even though there's a crash, Raymond doesn't wake.

They've never been travelling types, venturing only as far as Chilliwack, Hope, the Okanagan Valley – places they could drive to in a day. But eight months ago, after the doctors had told them they were stopping treatment, they had gone to England for the first time. Raymond had been fascinated by early medieval England since his university days and he begged to see the burial mounds of the Anglo-Saxon pagans, still visible after 1,500 years. "The extravagance. Sometimes, entire ships were buried."

Vince hadn't at all been sure about Sutton Hoo. For all its archaeological significance and similarities to Beowulf's landscape, Sutton Hoo was essentially a graveyard, a monument to memory, and wasn't that a bit maudlin given the circumstances? "But don't forget," Raymond said, "Beowulf was a hero who proved his strength against impossible odds." He winked. "Can't you see the resemblance?"

In the visitor's centre, Raymond looked at the famous masked helmet found in one of the burial mounds: so seemingly insubstantial, just a rusted piece of iron with two holes where the eyes would have been. "It looks so small," he said. "You think he was a small man?"

"Maybe. People were smaller back then. Poor nutrition."

Raymond leaned closer to the glass case. "It's hard to believe a man once wore that. Did he have children? Who was he? How did he die? Was he happy? All lost, you know." He pulled away from the glass case and turned to Vince. "What happens to stories like that?"

"Like what?"

"Peoples' stories. Their lives. People fall into the timeline and then fall out again. What happens to things they leave behind?"

"If you're lucky, you have kids that don't throw it all out, or sell it and vacation in Florida with the money. Maybe they keep your records or books. Or maybe it ends up in a museum like this."

"I'm not talking about *artefacts*. They're almost meaningless." He rubbed his eyes, something he always did when trying to clarify something in his mind. "Take our loft, for instance. It used to be a glass factory. It was a place where

people worked and talked and maybe fell in love. A secretary
and one of the truck drivers, let's say. Maybe our living room
is where their romance blossomed. So they have their first
kiss there. Then let's pretend they get married and have
babies. So what happens to that?"

"To what? You said. They have a baby."

"No, the *moment* of the kiss. It existed. Then it was gone.
What happens to that moment? Where does it go? Is there
some kind of eternal tome, a repository of events? Is someone keeping a record of them? Is there someone who knows
what happened to everyone? Even saying something like
'they kissed' seems so stupid and reductive. One day our
living room won't exist anymore. But that doesn't make what
it was or what happened in it any less real, does it? Is there
a word for that? What do you call something that no longer
exists in reality?"

Vince thought about it and after a long pause said, "A
memory."

Raymond lowered his head. His breathing was loud and
laboured. "*Memory* is not the right word. It's deeper than
that. Besides, what about when those memories are gone.
What do you call it then? The moment of the kiss when no
one remembers it?"

Vince had chewed a hole in his lip. Raymond had to stop
working himself up. He put his arm around Raymond's
shoulder. "You hungry?"

"I want to remember everything. Thing is, I don't even
remember what I had for breakfast." He laughed dryly.

That evening, they had returned to their hotel and made
love. He remembers how they took their time. They were

slow and gentle with each other, their lips full of hunger and tenderness.

While Raymond continues to sleep off the effect of the morphine, Vince sits in the wingback chair, masturbating. Two weeks of pressure explodes into Vince's climax, bringing him a temporary release.

He shuffles to the kitchen and picks up a dish rag, hard and crusty from hanging over the faucet, and after he wipes himself with it he notices his hand smells like bleach. He tosses the rag into the garbage can under the sink. It looks suspicious, so he hides it under some plastic food wrappers. He turns on the faucet and lets the water rinse what's left of his traces down the drain.

"Woodlands," Raymond says, waking up, as though continuing a conversation from earlier. "We're going to Woodlands tomorrow."

"What for?"

"I might not be well enough to go later."

"I don't know if that's such a good idea right now." Vince doesn't say in your state.

"Nestor says all the dead are buried there."

"Does Nestor think you should go?" Vince asks defensively.

"No. He doesn't think it's a good idea, either."

"But *you* want to."

"Yes. To help Charlie." Raymond confesses that for weeks now, the ghost has paced the floor of their bedroom nightly like a man looking for something he's lost. "A hopping ghost," Lucille had called it, the first and still only time she had come to visit them. A *po*. A ghost without a tomb of its own. "That's why I can't sleep."

Raymond turns over in bed and sighs. As the light shining in from the window falls onto his half-closed eyes, he looks strangely at peace, resigned. "Maybe I deserve it."

It was at Sutton Hoo where Raymond told him something he'd never said out loud, but which Vince had suspected for years. Leaning over the masked helmet, Raymond confessed he felt responsible for his father's death. Though the doctors called it heart disease, Raymond said, "I know what it really was. He died of disappointment. Heart disease is really just a broken heart."

Is that what Raymond believes? That Charlie has been sent to punish him because he didn't live up to his father's expectations?

Vince can't stand the self-pitying look on Raymond's face. He can't say no. He sits beside him on the bed. "If you want to go, then it's up to you, not Nestor."

Then he adds, "Besides, if it turns out ghosts are real, it means you can come back and haunt me." He says it as a joke and doesn't expect the hard knot in his throat.

Raymond looks at him. He says nothing for a moment and then, unexpectedly, he smiles. He begins to rub Vince's shoulder. "Of course I'll haunt you, baby, of course I'll haunt you."

The next day, Nestor insists on accompanying them. He insists on bundling Raymond into a sweater and a hat with ear flaps and pushing his wheelchair down to the car park.

"You don't have to come," Vince says.

"The more the many-er," Nestor says. "What are friends are for?"

In the car park, Nestor gives Raymond a notebook and some drawing pencils for some art-therapy practice before getting into the car.

Once on the road, Vince smiles, obstinately hopeful. He reminds himself to cherish the small victories, like having Raymond out of the house, by his side. This moment is all they have. Though Raymond prefers to muse about the past, Vince knows the present is what matters. Raymond may wonder about what happens to things that fall out of the timeline, but time doesn't exist on a line. It pops, Vince thinks, in a series, flashes of present followed by flashes of present and so on to infinity: a whole field of fireflies. Now you see them, now you don't.

What if they can't find the grave? What if there's no headstone to touch or to pull dandelions away from or to leave the carnations they've brought with them? But he doesn't say anything to Raymond about his concerns. Who is he to take away Raymond's hope?

As they drive down East Columbia, Raymond draws a picture in the passenger seat, spiral binder and graphite pencils on his lap. He is sketching a self-portrait. The cellophane wrapper around the pink carnations crunches as Nestor shifts in the back seat.

"You're no artist."

"Genius is so often scorned," Raymond says.

By the time they get to Woodlands, Raymond has finished his picture. It's not a self-portrait but a sketch of someone who looks strangely like him, but not how he looks now, nor how he used to look. He's smudged the graphite outline of the face and body so that the man in the picture looks as though he's underwater, his edges blurred, the way a pebble might look at the bottom of a fast-moving stream.

"Who's that?" Vince asks, taking the keys out of the ignition.

Nestor helps Raymond get out of the car and into his wheelchair. "It's not very good, is it? It started out as Charlie, but it doesn't look like him at all." Raymond puts the sketch under his arm.

In the bright sunlight, Raymond points to something on Nestor's cheek, a small cut.

Nestor shrugs. "A patient. He threw a candy dish at me because he thought I was stealing from him."

For the first time, Vince thinks of Nestor in other people's houses. It surprises him he's never pictured this before. Or wondered about Nestor's other clients, what he has to contend with.

"That's *terrible*," Raymond says. "Promise me you won't go back there."

Nestor nods noncommittally.

"Promise?"

They begin to walk toward the main building, Vince pushing the wheelchair, the handles slippery in his sweating hands.

Derelict buildings brood in the fierce sun. In contrast to the ragged lawn, a cheerful billboard on the site of the old hospital announces the coming of new condos.

"Are we there yet?" Raymond asks.

"Getting close," answers Nestor.

Vince looks from one side of the field to the other bordered by old-growth firs, his gaze sweeping over the rolling, manicured lawn. "You worked here?"

"It wasn't a bad place," Nestor says, "all the time."

"I remember watching it close on the news — what was that, three or four years ago now?"

"It's pretty here," Raymond says, looking around. A pool, filled by a stream flowing downward from a hill is flanked by a grove of trees.

Vince tries to shake off the goose bumps on his arms. There's something tactile about the stillness that hovers eerily over the grassy expanse.

Nestor, too, is looking around. His head pivots left and right while creases grow on his brow.

"I don't understand," Nestor says. "I — this is where the cemetery should be."

"So where is it?"

"That's what I'm trying to tell you. It's not here."

The tires of Raymond's wheelchair sink into the soft lawn as they push forward under the sun, looking for a grave marker, a map mounted on an information board, a sign. A hundred yards away, a woman in exercise pants picks up her poodle's feces with a plastic bag. Vince leaves Raymond and Nestor resting under a tree so he can make better time searching on his own. "You're probably just disoriented. It's been a long time," he says to Nestor. "I'll be right back. Stay here with Raymond."

Vince has only been walking for a few minutes when he comes to a grove of willow trees and stubs his toe. The pain crackles up his foot and, kneeling to rub his toe, he looks down. Next to his foot lies a headstone covered in brush. Confused, he moves to the next tree, a weeping elm, under which more headstones lay in grim disorder, nearly invisible beneath its draped branches.

After he leads Nestor and Raymond back to his grim discovery, he lifts a corner of the stone, holds it up for them to see.

Nestor is silent. Pushing Raymond's wheelchair closer he mouths the words, "Oh, no."

Some gravestones have been stacked and stored one on top of the other. No human attempt has been made to hide them, only nature has rendered them partially hidden beneath fallen leaves, long grass. Vince finds others piled in a nearby garden shed.

"I want to go in with you," Raymond says.

"The wheelchair, it won't fit through the door," Nestor says.

"I want to."

"I don't think that's a good idea," Nestor says. Still, he lets Raymond get out of his wheelchair slowly and walks closely behind him, watchful, ready to catch him if he falls, as he shuffles toward the shed, thin in his leather jacket. Once Raymond is stationed inside the shed with Vince, Vince helps Raymond get as comfortable as he can, seated atop a blanket, resting with his back against the wall. The air is damp and smells of earthworms, moss, and wood. Vince hopes the air is not too cold for Raymond.

Through the open doorway, Vince can see Nestor outside, shuffling through the back pack, getting out drinking boxes and sandwiches for their lunch. Vince kneels and puts his hand on the flat surface of a gravestone, the first of many, piled up like cord wood. He brushes off the dead leaves to read: Lewis? – something. The caked dust crumbles off the cast concrete as he caresses the grooves.

He lifts the stone. It's heavier than he expected and his back twinges as he turns to set it apart from the pile. The stones smell of urine: local dogs must have roamed these grounds freely for years. He brushes off dried worms. Then he does the same for the next one. Each stone once memorialised a face, a name, a story.

The stones *clack* as Vince builds a new stack. They are sometimes difficult to balance on top of each other as some of the stones have been split in two with one half lost, while others have been battered by the years and neglect to mere shards that fall to the ground. The concrete feels moist and leaves a chalky residue on his hands, stealing the warmth from his palms.

Vince drifts between tears and anger. They spend most of the afternoon in that garden shed, looking through the tombstones, more than three hundred of them. Nestor comes in and out asking if they want more sandwiches or apples or granola bars.

"I'm going to leave this for Charlie," Raymond says, opening his hand, a carved wooden turtle in his palm. "Nestor got it for me in Chinatown. Do you like it?"

Vince holds his head aloof, fights to stop himself from looking down his nose at it.

"The turtle. He holds the world on his back."

Vince doesn't acknowledge the remark. It's enough that he has to accept Raymond's high estimation of Nestor. He brushes the dirt off another of the gravestones, moving his hand softly over the letters, touching them as gently as a lover. A shudder passes through him, a sudden strange presentiment of loss, a nostalgia for the present. "I feel like I'm going crazy."

Raymond laughs. "Look at me. I'm being visited by dead people."

They leave the garden shed, Raymond with his turtle and pencil drawing clutched in his hand, Vince steadying him with an arm at his elbow, and they walk out onto the grass.

"If you are going a long way, go slowly," Nestor says.

With Raymond leaning heavily on his arm, they walk for a time, the sun shifting behind clouds, the air growing still. They walk on the grass where the gravestones have been pulled like teeth from the rolling hills. There is nothing to acknowledge that more than three thousand bodies, according to Nestor, still lay underfoot. Vince blinks hard, looking over the grassy expanse, imagining what lies beneath.

When they approach the ridgeline of trees on the hill, they stop. Raymond crouches down and, next to the turtle, arranges the carnations, as well the picture he has drawn, over top of one of the many unmarked graves, laying them all on the grass. Then he folds at the waist, collapsing toward the ground, his cheek against the earth. Alarmed, Vince reaches out for him. "Honey?" He shakes his shoulder. He worries Raymond has passed out. But Raymond, his cheek still pressed firmly on the ground, opens one eye and peers up at Vince with a look of annoyance. "What?" he says.

"What are you doing?"

"Shhh. I'm listening." He closes his eyes again, presses his forehead to the ground.

Vince leaves him there and waits. He paces back and forth, biting at his fingernails, peeling the cuticles back with his teeth until they are raw. He wonders what Raymond hears, and what he himself might hear if he could only bring himself to lie down next to Raymond, press his own cheek into the solid earth, and listen.

By the time they get to Jericho Park later that afternoon it is raining. The grey sky hangs over the evergreens. Damp sea air invades Vince's flimsy windbreaker, a blue relic from the eighties which he refuses to get rid of, and seeps through the leather of his loafers, soaking his toes. He would rather be at home with a cup of Earl Grey on his lap, but it was his idea to stop in and visit Lucille, part of his ongoing peace mission, the all-or-nothing salvage operation into which he'll gladly sink his own heart.

"Not stay long, okay?" Nestor says, for which Vince is grateful.

Raymond's mother sits on a chair behind a table of bocce merchandise: clothing, ball rentals, and a metal box for the tournament entry fee. Vince pushes Raymond's wheelchair around the table, ducking under team lists that are hung with clothespins from the streamer above her, while Nestor walks at Raymond's side, holding the umbrella over him. Only when Raymond is in front of her does she get up from her chair and hug him.

"Hey, Mom," Raymond says, his eyes glassy from the morphine drip and fatigue.

Vince nods toward Nestor. "Lucille, this is Nestor. Nestor, Lucille."

"You want a T-shirt?" she asks Nestor. "Good cause. Charity for kids."

"We're not staying long," Vince says.

"I'm here until four. It's good to leave the house, you know? I like to help out."

"Helping out *is* good," Vince says. Does she hear the edge in his voice? Vince jams his fists into the kangaroo pouch of his windbreaker and feels some balled up Kleenex. His exhaustion from the early morning and his lack of sleep feels like a tight band around his head.

Nestor tucks and re-tucks the blanket around Raymond's knees.

"Nestor," Raymond says, "stop fussing."

"Check it out," Vince says, touching Raymond's elbow.

A man in a shirt that says "FBI, Full-Blooded Italian" steps up to the pitch, the weight of the shiny grapefruit-sized metal ball resting solidly in one palm. The mood is intense as the audience waits for the man to hit the other ball on the terrain with a resounding *puh-tank*.

"So. What is it today, Lucille? Who's the money for?" Vince asks.

Raymond's mother says nothing, simply points to multiple banners strung next to the team lists just to the right of his head. "Oh, geez," he says, angry at her condescension, though he's embarrassed he hadn't noticed. It's a symptom, he thinks, of how much he lives in his head these days. "Commercial Co-operative Centre. Kids Up Front Fundraiser. The Bocce Father Tournament." The last banner features a silhouette of Marlon Brando puffing a cigar. "That's just great," Vince says.

"Yah, I buy T-shirt," Nestor says.

"Black or white T-shirt?" she asks Nestor. "And this one with the Bocce Father, or just words?" She shuffles under the table. "I don't think I have bags. I did have bags. What did I do with them?"

Why won't she look at Raymond? Why does his sickness make her so uncomfortable? Why isn't Raymond upset that she is ignoring him? Instead, Raymond is tucking the shirt Nestor has bought him under his arm like a football, smiling his tired smile. Sometimes, he really does act like a man who believes he deserves his punishment.

Vince takes an egg-sized piece of concrete from his pocket and offers it to Lucille.

"What is it?" she says.

"Something I thought you might be interested in."

He knows he's goading her but he can't help it.

She takes it and before Vince can tell her it is a piece of a gravestone, the sun gleams through a break in the clouds and the park is illuminated, spotlighting the ancient beauty of the old-growth Douglas firs, their slick boughs, the game of bocce on the grass. A few people *oooh*, rub their arms, lift their faces to the light. For an instant the day is glorious.

"Look," Nestor says, pointing at the sun, "it's a blessing in the sky."

With the chunk of concrete in her hand, Lucille looks like a woman on the verge of some kind of action. Vince wonders what she is waiting for.

In that moment, with the sun glancing off Lucille's face, Vince begins to understand there are truths one speaks and others one doesn't. Maybe Lucille is waiting for a confession. Maybe she needs to hear her son say, "I'm sorry," before she can move on, grant forgiveness, and be forgiven herself.

Everyone has something to confess. Vince's confession is the tragedy of his infinitely small mind. His inability to believe in anything beyond himself, beyond what his puny eyes can see. He could never have joined Raymond down on the grass, honouring the unmarked dead with his cheek pressed to the ground.

And no matter how much love they share between them, Vince can't even begin to imagine what the world looks like through Raymond's eyes. To have faith. Vince has only his own pair of eyes through which to view everything for all eternity.

Vince looks at Lucille – like him, all she has left is Raymond. He feels the loneliness engulf him. She is poised and ready, but still waiting. He tries to imagine what kind of a push she needs. What they both need to let go.

"We went to Woodlands today," he tries. He doesn't know what to expect with this revelation.

Lucille pauses. "And?"

"Nothing much there," Vince says. "Most of it's been torn down."

She puts her hands on her lap. "I guess that's a good thing. Who wants to be reminded of the bad that happened. Negative energy. That's why I heard they're getting rid of everything, clearing the whole site." Then she forces a jovial tone. "You kids. Always up to something."

"We should go," Vince says.

"Already?" Raymond asks.

"I love you, don't complain."

"So soon?" Lucille says, flatly. It is a statement, not a request for them stay. Or does Vince detect a note of regret in her voice?

"But the sun just came out," Raymond says.

"Long day, you," Nestor agrees.

"Sometimes the best time to leave a party is when it's in full swing," Vince says. "Before all the mess."

Lucille smiles. "Okay. Gotcha." She makes a gun from her fingers and pretends to shoot them. "We see you soon, okay?"

Vince says okay, even though he knows it won't be soon or maybe ever again. For all he knows, this glimpse of Lucille, sitting at her table in a sunbeam, her hair like a blackberry, her face tilted upward, might be his last of her, and Raymond's last, too.

The wet grass, sparkling with raindrops, makes the wheelchair tires slip.

When they're halfway to the car they hear Lucille call out, "The stone." She's holding up the piece of concrete. "What do I do with it?"

Vince and Raymond share a look. Save the conversation for next time? Run back and tell her what it is? "Keep it," Vince calls back.

She's still holding the concrete with a puzzled grin.

"Should we go back and explain?" Raymond asks.

"It's nothing that can't wait," Vince says. "We'll do it another time."

Vince has been considering taking a leave of absence so he can stay home with Raymond full-time, although Raymond insists that's the last thing he wants. "Let's keep everything as normal as possible, okay? For as long as we can." So today Vince gives Raymond a shave in bed with the electric razor. His skin colour seems to change each week, from white to yellow to green. His lips are cracked and Vince has to shave around the eruptions. When he's done, he retrieves Raymond's makeup bag from the bathroom. But he forgets the comb. Then he forgets the hairspray.

"Quit it," Raymond says. "You're pacing as bad as Charlie." But there's no disapproval, only tenderness, in his voice.

Vince applies concealer around Raymond's eyes and brushes mascara onto his thinning lashes.

"How about some falsies – those ones made of feathers," Raymond says.

"I'm not sure about the chemical composition of the glue. Let's check with Nestor first."

"*Joking,*" Raymond says, giving a weak chuckle.

What do you say to someone who is dying? What words do you use and in what tense? Though they have never stopped planning for things and talking about the future, some days Vince feels like a liar.

Yet last night Vince dreamed he was nursing Raymond, much like he is now. Then he looked at his hands, noticed them for the first time as they hovered above his lover's face, mascara wand poised over his granite-coloured eyes. The hands were those of an old man, liver-spotted, wrinkled, arthritic. *Good God*, he'd wanted to cry. *Look how old we've grown.*

ACKNOWLEDGEMENTS

I would like to thank the following people:

For reading early drafts of these and other stories, Audrey McClellan, Sarah Selecky, Jody Gardner, and Yvette Guigueno. For their support, Yvette Guigueno, as well as Terry Glavin, Jeremy and Sus Borsos, Amanda Jardine, Jessica Kluthe, Peter Boychuk, and Michael Nardone. Thank you also to David Thanh, Landon James, Dan Hogg, Valerie Tenning, and Cliff Haman (for always answering my questions). Tim Lilburn, for introducing me to the phrase "nostalgia for the present" and "presentiment of loss"; Ibet Falk, who shared her swimming lessons with me; and rockabilly legend Art Adams, for the story about his white shoes.

For their inspiration, Earl Andersen, author of *Hard Place to Do Time*; Reverend Joseph B. Ingle, for *Last Rights*; Jack Hodgins, for *A Passion for Narrative*; Harold Brodkey, for *This Wild Darkness: The Story of My Death*; Sherwin B. Nuland, for *How We Die: Reflections on Life's Final Chapter*; and Jean MacNeil, for her story "Bethlehem." Thank you to Vancouver historian Lani Russwurm, and a deep and sincere thank you to Chris Yorath for his excellent book, *A Measure of Value*, without which my story "Floating Like the Dead" wouldn't exist.

Thank you to the Canada Council for the Arts, the British Columbia Arts Council, and the Social Sciences and Humanities Research Council for funding while writing these stories.

Thank you Jason Jobin, Helga Thorson, Lorna Jackson, John Gould, Bill Gaston, Gudrun Will, my Spanish expert Dan Russek, Florence Daurelle, and the members of my University of Victoria writing workshops. For their comments and suggestions, special thanks to Grant Buday, James Marshall, and Zsuzsi Gartner, as well as to Steven Price for the assignment he gave me that led to the Journey Prize.

Without my tireless editor, Anita Chong, these stories would not be what they are, and I thank her for always demanding my best. Thank you to Denise Bukowski, keeper of the faith.

My children, Jet and Maisie, for tolerating their "just-a-minute" Mommy. And no acknowledgement would be complete without my mentioning my husband, Hank, whose Indian head I stole; to whom I owe my sanity and my successes, however big or small; who loves me for better or for worse. Thank you, with all my heart, for making each day beautiful, possible, and worthwhile.